Lies in the Dark

Agnes H. Hagadus

PublishAmerica
Baltimore

First printing

ISBN: 1-4137-5602-6
PUBLISHED BY PUBLISHAMERICA, LLLP
www.publishamerica.com
Baltimore

Printed in the United States of America

This is to all the people that have believed in me, including all of my co-workers who took the time to read my writing and give me the strength to go on. And for those out there that know, my faithful readers of my internet publishing. That is what started it all, and without your kind words, I may never have had the courage to try my own work and now succeed. For that, I will be eternally grateful.

The full moon was only half showing behind a bevy of dark grey clouds. Walking down an alley at three in the morning was not unusual for the tall dark-haired man. It was unusual that his eleven-year-old daughter was with him. But it had been a special day. It was her birthday and they had gone to a basketball game. Her favorite college team had been playing the local one. It was a rare opportunity that he actually had the day off and that he could take his little girl. The game had gone into double overtime and that is why the two were now walking down the empty alleyway at the early hour.

Or at least it appeared to be empty. The man kept looking around, peering into every shadow. His daughter looked up at him. She could sense his uneasiness. That was something that was really strange. Her father, after all, was a police officer and was not scared of anything. She had been assured of this many times.

The man caught the worried expression on his daughter's little face. "It's all right, darling." He squeezed her hand tightly. "It's just that I didn't think the game would last that long. And you've got school tomorrow." Again, he looked around. It was as if he could feel a presence and not one that he liked.

The little girl started to look around as well. If her father sensed something, there must be something in the shadows. After all, he was a very good cop. Her mother had told her this over and over again before she had died of cancer two years ago.

Two shadows walking behind a dumpster caught both of their attentions. The man pulled his daughter closer to his left side while placing his free right hand on the gun he had strapped to his hip. This was not the bad part of Lansing, Michigan, but one could never be too careful. Especially when you were in a dark alley at three in the morning.

The man and the little girl stood there for several minutes. There was not any movement in all that time. The man began wondering if he had imagined the whole thing. After all, the clouds floating over the full moon did not allow for much light. And this alley was, unfortunately, poorly lit.

A crash of garbage cans from behind them made them both turn quickly. Now standing in front of them was this gang. At least that is the best way the little girl could describe them. Even in the dim light she could see that their skin was pale, almost as pale as pure white snow. They were all dressed in black leather accentuating the paleness of their faces. One had a nose ring. Another wore a chain from his left ear to his nose. There were five in total.

"Well, if it isn't Mr. Good Guy Cop," the one with the nose ring said. "And what do we have here?" He smiled at the little girl who quickly wrapped herself around her father's leg. "Aww, don't worry, sweetheart. We're not gonna hurt you. Much."

"You leave her alone." The dark-haired man pulled out the gun that he always carried. "You and I will talk about this later. Don't involve the girl."

"Well, now." The guy with the nose ring took a couple steps forward. "I'd really like to do that. But you see, you haven't exactly been keeping up with your end of the bargain, now have you?" Mr. Nose Ring stepped even closer. "I'll take payment anyway that I can get. Even a little girl would be better than nothing."

Her father quickly put the little girl behind him. "She is not an option. If you continue to threaten her, our deal will be permanently off. I promise to finish our business by Monday. Please give me that long. And then we can go our separate ways."

Mr. Nose Ring turned back to his four followers who had stood silently watching the whole exchange. "What do you think, boys? Do you really think we can trust him?" He turned back around. He licked his lips as he looked at the little girl. "After all, payment was due more than three weeks ago. Am I really supposed to believe that you all of a sudden can come up with the goods? It's not looking so good. And you know you'll never really be free to go your separate way."

The gun in the man's hand started to shake. "Please, just let us go and I will make good. I promise. Just don't hurt my little girl."

"I think we say no to that option." Mr. Nose Ring lunged for the gun, easily knocking it out of his hand. "I'm faster than you can imagine. I am stronger, and guns have no effect on my kind. You forget what I am." As he was saying this, his teeth grew long, and his eyes began glowing a fiery orange. He now had fangs.

"Oh, God!" the man managed to squeak out. "Please don't hurt the girl."

Mr. Nose Ring nodded toward the girl. The others surrounded her. Her eyes grew wide with terror. She refused to take her eyes off her father. Maybe there was a way that she could help.

"I'm afraid you're just the dinner. She's the ever so sweet dessert." His teeth were in the man's neck before anything else could be said or done. The man's eyes widened. Slowly, his breathing came to a stop as his face turned paler and paler. Mr. Nose Ring pulled back, blood dripping from the corners of his mouth. Unceremoniously, he wiped the blood with the back of his hand and licked it clean.

The girl began crying. She saw the lifeless body of her father fall with a thud to the ground. Her body began shaking. The nose ring guy came straight for her. "You leave me alone, you son of a bitch."

"Well, well." He stopped in his tracks at her outburst. "Such language from a little girl. Now where on earth would you pick that up?" He smiled down at her.

"I'm not as innocent a-as I look." She could hardly get the words out her tears were coming so fast and so hard. "I know what you are. My daddy told me all about your kind. I'm not supposed to trust any of you. You're all bad."

"That's not necessarily true." A strong female voice caught everyone's attention. "Let her go. You took care of the one that wasn't holding up his end of the deal you had going."

"You!" The word hissed out of the nose ring guy. "I thought…"

"You think?" The female took several steps toward the group. "Why do I find that hard to believe? Maybe because I know who you are. I know your reputation."

"And what about yours?" He smiled in return. "Don't think I don't know about your reputation."

"I never worry about my reputation. People will think what they want of me." She took a few more steps closer. "Like I said, let her go." She pointed down to the little girl's father's lifeless body. "He knew not how to deal with our kind. I do. You might want to rethink the whole killing the girl thing. Or I may just get a little cranky."

Mr. Nose Ring simply laughed. "Am I really supposed to be threatened by one stupid female vampire?"

"I would be. You're new to the whole immortal life." She again took several steps closer to him. They were now only two feet apart. "Whereas I've been around since they believed the earth was flat." She tilted her head. "Even before I was granted immortal life, I never believed that. I was smarter than the average woman. And definitely smarter than the average man."

"And like a typical woman, you like to talk a whole lot. Too much." He shook his head. "This is getting really boring. What say we liven things up a little bit." He looked her up and down. "Would you care to share a dance with my boys?"

She smiled. "That would simply be my pleasure." The woman took a fighting stance. She waited for one of the others to make the first move. "I'm waiting. Take your best shot."

"Boys, show her how we like to dance." Mr. Nose Ring grabbed the little girl by the arm. "I'll watch our little dessert until you have shown this freak how to show the proper respect."

The four that had been surrounding the little girl began circling the woman. She kept herself still and in battle ready mode. The first one finally simply dove for her. She sidestepped him and tripped him, sending him into the garbage cans.

The remaining three attacked as one. The woman leapt into the air, doing a split and landing solid kicks on two of them. As she was landing, her closed fist landed on top of the third one's head. All four scrambled to their feet at the same time.

"If this is the best you guys can do, you really ought to rethink trying to be baddies." She laughed as she said it.

"You bitch!" The nose ring guy shoved the girl to the one that had the chain. "You watch the brat. I'll take care of this one myself."

"Oh, whatever shall I do? The big bad leader is going to show me how tough he is. I'm oh so scared." The female vampire shook her head. She growled low in her throat. A huge smile made its way onto her face. "Are you prepared for the final death?"

Mr. Nose Ring simply laughed. "I still say you're a typical woman. You talk too much."

"And you're a typical male." She smiled at him. "You think too little."

The male vampire growled as he launched himself at her. His fist connected with her chin. She was only slightly knocked back. But there was a little blood at the corner of her mouth. "I guess you're not as good as you think you are."

"Or maybe you're just as stupid as you look." She laughed as she pointed to his chest.

All he managed was, "How the… " She had managed to bury a wooden stake in his heart, just one of the few ways to kill a vampire. He was now simply a pile of dust slowly blowing around the darkened alleyway.

She took several steps toward the remaining vampires. "Now, you can all go home and be good little boys or I can take care of you as easily as your annoying leader. It's your choice."

The remaining four vampires looked at each other for a minute. The one with the chain let go of the girl and ran for the end of the alleyway. It did not take long for the remaining three to follow.

The little girl stood wide-eyed, staring at the person or thing that had just saved her. The woman was dressed in black leather as well. Her long dark hair was slightly blowing in the breeze. She had the darkest eyes that the girl had ever seen.

The little girl took two steps toward the woman. Out of the corner of her eye, she again saw the lifeless body of her father. She ran over to him and began crying again. She laid her body across his.

The woman slowly came up behind her. "I know this isn't easy. I'm sorry for your loss. We've got to call someone. Do you have any family?"

9

Finally, the little girl managed to stand back up. She looked into those dark eyes. "W-why did you save me?"

"It's what I do." She looked down at the girl's father. "I'm just sorry that I couldn't have come sooner. If I had, maybe...." She let out a little growl. The little girl took several steps back. "I'm sorry. Even though I've chosen the path of good, I sometimes have a little trouble controlling the inner beast. Think of it as a bad temper, only with not so good consequences should I ever lose control."

The girl stepped closer again. She had a little half smile showing on her face. "I-I'm just wondering what's going to happen now. Daddy's gone; Momma died when I was nine. I'm all alone."

The woman's dark eyes widened. "You don't have anyone?" The little girl shook her head. "No grandparents? Aunts, uncles? There's nobody?" The girl nodded, close to tears again. "Oh, crap." The woman began pacing. That was when the red and blue lights began flashing at the end of the alleyway.

"Hold it right there, don't move." A bright light fixed on the woman.

She held up her hands and did not move a muscle. Whispering, she said, "We can't tell them what really happened." The girl stared at her. "They won't believe you or me about vampires, even though I am one. You can tell it sorta like it happened. But just say they were a gang on drugs, all right?"

The girl nodded. She whispered back, "I understand." Two uniformed officers quickly came toward them. Before they got too close, the girl again whispered, "I know them. They are friends of Daddy's. Let me do the talking."

"My, God!" The first officer was by the little girl's side. "Are you all right, sweetie?" She tried not to start crying yet again. "What exactly happened?"

"They got Daddy."

It was two days later. The same little girl was cleaning out her bedroom that she could no longer stay in. She was now going to have to stay with the Andersons. They would be her foster family, at least for a little while. From what she had heard of the whole thing, a lot of kids bounced from home to home. She so was not looking forward to this.

There was a tap at her bedroom window. She looked up to see the mysterious woman who had saved her two days ago. It was unfortunate that she had been too late to save her father as well. A big smile made it to her face as she opened the window.

"Where you off to, kid?" The woman smiled.

"They're making me go to some foster home." She let out a huge sigh. "From what others have told me, I won't be there for long. I don't think I'll ever have a real home again."

"Would it make you feel better if I told you I'd be keeping an eye on you, no matter where you end up?" Her smile grew even larger.

"That would be cool." The little girl leaned out the window and gave her a great big hug. Suddenly, she pulled back. "Not to sound ungrateful, but why?"

"That's a good question." She looked into the little girl's brown eyes. "Let's just say that I think you're special. And that someday you're going to be even more special." She shrugged. "What can I say? You're a pain in the ass. But I like you. I like you a lot."

The little girl laughed. She stopped suddenly. "Haven't done that since he died." Tears quickly formed in the corner of her eyes. "Sorry. Every time I even think about him, I see him lying there in the alley. His body so still and pale. It makes me want to throw up and cry and scream, all at the same time."

"It's going to. For a long time." The woman put her hand on the girl's shoulder. "Take it from somebody that's been around a while. It will get better. It just takes time."

"If you say so." The girl sighed heavily.

"And in the meantime, just know I'll always be watching over you." She handed the girl a card. "That has my cell phone number on it. If you ever need anything, just call."

The girl stared at the card. It did not have a name or address. Just the phone number. "But..." By the time she looked back up, the woman was gone. She was on her own now, with only a mysterious stranger watching over her.

"Miss Freemont?" the loud persistent female voice said for the third time.

The thirty-year-old sandy blonde looked up. "Yes?" She shook her head. "I'm sorry. I kinda got lost in thought. That happens from time to time. You were saying?"

"Yes, well." The petite black-haired woman of about fifty glanced around the office. It was not in the better part of Lansing, Michigan. The best way to describe the surroundings would be pre-condemned. It amazed her that the offices were allowed to remain open. "I was wanting you to look into my husband's death." She handed the other woman a photo. "This is a picture that I got from the coroner's office. It doesn't really go with what the final cause of death was listed as."

Miss Freemont looked at the picture. Her eyes widened. She knew exactly how the man had died. There was no way that some gang member poked two little holes in the man's neck and left him there to bleed to death. It had been a long time since she had come across a vampire attack. It made her wonder if there was not a reason for this fresh, or should she say dead, blood being in town.

She looked up at the woman standing in front of her. Even though she had offered her a chair, the woman had refused. It irritated her when people thought that they were better than others. And that is exactly how it felt. The woman wanted to look down on her. "I think I already know what happened, Mrs. Claymore. But I'm not sure if you'll believe me or not. Hardly anybody believes the things that I know are facts."

Mrs. Claymore shook her head. "Miss Freemont…"

"I've told you, call me Andrea." She smiled at the woman.

"Andrea." She nodded. "As I was going to say, you seem to be talking in riddles. Do you really know what happened to my husband? And if so, how, without even so much as investigating?"

"It's because I've come across this many times in my thirty years of life." She eyed the older woman very carefully. "What if I were to tell you that vampires are real?"

Mrs. Claymore burst out laughing. "Indeed. That is just ridiculous. Do you really expect me to believe that the monsters that did this to my Harry are some demons? Really."

Andrea shook her head. "I told you that you probably wouldn't believe me. But I believe it's true. I can ask around if you want. But all signs are pointing to a new vampire gang in town." She shook her head. "I'd heard about another attack two days ago. But my source isn't very reliable. I only listen to half of what he has to say. He's usually too drunk to believe the other half."

Now Mrs. Claymore was pacing. "You know, my dear. If you didn't want to take my case and my considerable money, you could have just said so. Instead, you come up with these fanciful ideas that vampires are real. Let me guess, everything I've ever feared is real as well?"

"You got it." Andrea tried to smile. She knew that she had lost this client the minute she had said the word *vampire*. Nobody wanted to accept that there were undead monsters out there. What most people did not realize was that not all of them were evil. Just like the few demons she had come across. Some were as bad as they get, and others would not harm a fly.

"Really, this is all too much." Mrs. Claymore stormed out the door, slamming it behind her. The door rattled on its hinges it hung so loosely.

The door slowly opened again. Standing there was a freckled face blue-eyed blonde man. He was only about twenty years old and wore glasses, definitely a stereotypical geek. He smiled sheepishly at Andrea. "I take it that we don't have a client, boss?"

Andrea smiled back. "Yeah, well, I had to go and be honest with her. You know how people can't handle the truth. Especially little old biddies like her."

"You mentioned the V word I take it." He chuckled softly to himself. "That does do it every time, doesn't it?" He glanced back out the door.

"What is it, Adam?" She knew he had something to share. He just did not want to at the moment.

"It may be bad timing, but your first interview is here." Andrea raised her eyes as if asking a question. "You know, for the computer expert person."

"Oh, right." She looked at the picture that Mrs. Claymore had left behind. "Let me get this taken care of. Five minutes, then send him in."

"Uh," Adam started to squirm. Andrea looked up at him. "It's a-a woman." He quickly shut the door.

Andrea shook her head. That was the last type of distraction she needed. She had specifically asked that only males be allowed to apply for the hacker position. She did not want to even try not to have a relationship at this moment. Since she was gay, being around men meant no chance of getting into one.

She quickly slipped the picture into a manilla folder that was already labeled "Claymore." She made some notes inside the folder and put the file in the drawer of her desk. By the time she had done all this, there was a knock on the door.

Adam's voice came from the other side. "Are you ready, Miss Freemont?"

"Call me Andrea, and send in the first victim." She shuffled more of the papers on her desk. The door opened and closed. She did not bother looking up. She just said, "Please, have a seat." The sound of the chair scraping on the floor made her look up.

A redheaded woman with glasses was pulling the chair closer to her desk. Andrea could not help but stare at the woman. It had been a long time since she had seen anyone so beautiful, even if it was in a slightly nerdy way. She watched her finally settle the chair in front of the desk. The woman sat so very ladylike.

It took a few minutes for Andrea to find her voice. "Sorry. Just thinking about my latest case." The woman handed her some papers that turned out to be her resume. Andrea's eyes widened at the vast amount of experience the woman already had. She had worked for some of the best companies in Lansing and a few others across the United States. "So, Miss Walker."

"Please, call me Alicia, Miss Freemont." Alicia smiled a huge smile.

"Only if you call me Andrea." The woman nodded her head in agreement. "Not to sound ungrateful, but why on earth would somebody as talented, and I assume sought after, want to work for a private detective?" She motioned around the room. "And as you can probably tell, I'm sorta what they would call low rent, meaning I won't be able to pay you a whole lot."

Alicia shrugged. "I've done the working for the so-called best or most prestigious companies. It's way overrated. And boring as hell." Andrea raised her eyebrows at the tone and word usage. "Listen, Andrea, I'm not as sweet and innocent as I look." She pointed to the paper in front of her. "I have done some things, unofficially, for people. That was more interesting and fun."

Andrea could not help but laugh. "Well, that's a very good attitude to have in this business. I'm not saying I do it a lot, but there are times when you kinda have to bend the rules. Things don't always get done unless you do."

"I couldn't agree more." Alicia pointed to the paper. "If you look at the back, you'll see what I mean, in more detail."

Andrea turned the paper over. There was a list of two separate jail times that the woman across from her had served. All of them had to do with breaking into the City of Lansing's mainframe computer.

"It appears you do know how to get around the rules." Andrea looked up at her. "You just have to be a little more careful when it comes to getting caught."

"Let's just say that the first time was me being overly confident. The second, I was just a little careless." She smiled. "I've definitely learned from my past mistakes. You can count on me, if you feel you can hire me, not to mess up again."

"I like the sounds of that." Andrea again glanced over the resume. "I do like what I see." She blushed a little at the double meaning of the statement she had just said, not that Alicia would understand the second meaning, not yet anyway. It was her darn saying what she thought that often got her into trouble. She hoped that this was not one of those times. "I still have a couple other people to interview."

15

Alicia quickly stood. "I understand. I'm not exactly what you were looking for." She turned to go.

"Wait." Andrea quickly stood as well. "I just wanted to ask you something. You are this great computer genius, and you want to work for me and I can't pay much. Why?"

Alicia took a couple steps toward Andrea. She smiled big as she said, "I've heard a lot about you, Andrea. You do good, even when you don't always get paid for it." They were now standing inches away from one another. "I like your style. It meshes with mine. And I've always wanted to be more than just a 'hacker' as they call me. I want to do what you do."

"You want to be a private detective?" Andrea's eyes widened in surprise.

"Let's just say that there are reasons that I like digging into people's pasts." She shrugged. "You learn a lot about other people but also about yourself." She took Andrea's hand in hers. "I think we've said all we need to say. I hope you'll hire me. It feels like it could be really fun working with you. In a lot of different ways." She quickly turned and walked out the door.

Andrea stared after the redhead. She could not believe her ears. The woman not only wanted to work for her for practically nothing, but she was also coming on to her. That just could not be. It had to have been her imagination. Women just did not hit on plain Janes like her. Hell, men did not even usually try anything with her. It had to be wishful thinking.

Her thoughts were interrupted by Adam knocking on the door frame. "Earth to boss. Is anybody home?"

Andrea shook her head. "Forget the rest of the interviews. Hire that woman and now."

Adam crinkled up his forehead. "But I thought you said…"

"Never mind what I said." Andrea turned her back on him. "That is the person for this job. In every single way."

16

The black-haired woman stood in the shadows of the building. She was careful not to let the bright morning sun shine on her. While listening to the whole conversation, a feeling had crept over her. It was not something she liked, not one bit.

In addition, there was the matter that Mrs. Claymore had brought up. There was indeed a new vampire gang in town. It was already causing several problems, ones that her charge could not possibly understand. Her charge only thought of the good versus evil, she forgot about the gray areas. And how sometimes the good crossed over to the bad.

She turned and opened the manhole cover. Once she was in far enough, she slid the cover back to its original spot. There was total darkness in the sewer. But her eyes could see. It was one of the many advantages of being a vampire. She had greater hearing and seeing senses and an increased strength. Besides, she did not have to breathe, which came in handy for someone that traveled in the sewers to avoid the sunlight.

It did not take long for her to make it back to her lair. She had very few amenities. There was only a refrigerator to keep the blood she got from various butchers fresh, a small television to try to keep up with current events, and a small day bed. She really did not require sleep, but if she were injured in a fight, it helped her healing powers if she did so.

There were also all the tools for dealing with her kind. The shelves were lined with bottle after bottle of holy water. On specially made hooks hung several wooden stakes. She also had several swords of varying sizes. Those were good for beheading. She could not keep garlic with her like she told her charge to. But she did have a mini blowtorch. She was always careful when she used that. After all, she could easily set herself on fire and she would finally be truly dead.

She had not told her charge her age, but she was now more than six hundred years old. All the vampires that had been turned when she had been were long ago dead. Even her sire was nothing but dust. He had come across her while she was taking yet another beating from her master.

In those days, a woman was to be silent, especially a woman who was nothing more than a slave. But she had been born with more knowledge than most of the men around her. She had trouble keeping her mouth shut. It had lead to many beatings over her twenty years of life.

Hector had watched the whole scene unfold before him. She had indeed shown up her master in front of his peers. In those times, she was lucky to only be receiving a beating. She could very well have been killed for such an offense. Hector had scared off all those in attendance by baring his fangs.

She herself had been terrified of him. But instead of harming her, he had taken her to his home. He had helped her heal. It took several weeks because the beating had been so severe. Finally, when she was at full strength again, he offered her a choice. She could go on living the life she had and probably would be dead by the time she was twenty-five.

Or she could let him give her the strength he possessed. She would never again have to suffer such beatings. She would have to learn to adapt to the times that were always changing. Not really understanding what he was offering her, she had allowed him to drink of her and she then drank of him. He had turned her into a vampire.

It had been the strangest feeling as she had died. The world had entered a white blissful room. There was no feeling, no harm, nothing that she had ever feared or hated. But then, her eyes had opened again. She still felt all the things she had before, but she knew that there was no breath in her. And she now needed blood to survive.

Hector quickly explained to her that she was now a vampire who did indeed need blood to survive. But it did not need to be human's blood. Many of their compatriots did not care. They thought that eternal life meant that one could do as they pleased. They did not care about the consequences. Their souls had been taken, and nothing left in their place. He had been left with a conscience, almost like a soul.

But she did. She must also have a conscience hidden inside of her as well. As Hector had told her, the best way to survive an eternal life was to find a purpose. His was seeking out those that could not defend themselves and helping them. Just as he had helped her. He normally did not turn his charges like he did her. But he could sense something very special about her. He knew that she would use the gifts that he had granted her for good.

And she did. Although in these changing times, there was a grayer area surrounding good and evil. It was not always as clear as it once had been. Nothing in these modern times was as clear as it used to be.

And now she had another decision to make. Her charge was possibly in danger from this new person. She just could not be sure if it were true. But her instincts were telling her that all was not as it seemed. Of course, they were not with her, either.

If her charge ever found out the things she had done, she may not be able to readily accept them. In fact, her charge may very well come after her. It was not a pleasant thought. She loved her charge dearly. The thought that they would come to blows made her still heart ache. She knew that if it came down to herself and her charge, she would sacrifice herself.

Alicia pulled into the parking lot for the state library. She parked at the curb and acted as though she were waiting for somebody. After several minutes, she pulled out her cell phone. After punching a couple numbers, she hit the send button.

A deep male's voice was at the other end. "Did you succeed?"

"All too well." She looked around. A couple people were beginning to stare. "Listen. I'm going to have to get moving. What's the next part of the plan? Am I supposed to jump in bed with her right away or are we supposed to build up to that slowly? It'll be fun either way."

"Alicia!" the voice thundered in her ear. "You know I don't like that talk. I'm your father after all."

"Yeah, and you're asking me to do anything and anything to get in with this woman." She looked at the doors, trying to make it appear as if she could not understand why she was still waiting. "I still don't get what is so important about this woman. She is good looking, and she seems smart, but why do we need to be on the inside with this one?"

She could hear his deep sigh. "It is not always for you to understand why we do the things we do. Your orders still are the same. We don't have time to put another operative in place. Time is of the essence." He softly chuckled to himself. "Besides, you are the one that has the talents for this particular job."

Finally looking like she was frustrated, she pulled out of the parking lot and headed toward her apartment on Kalamazoo Street. Looking frustrated was not that hard. She was not liking the conversation she was having with her father. "Do you mean my computer skills or the fact that I've been known to have my way with the ladies?"

"Alicia!" Her father scowled at the other end of the phone. "You know how I hate all this talk of your supposed lifestyle. I still say you've chosen this life just to irritate me."

"That's right, Dad. I'm a big ole lesbian just to get you going." She chuckled softly. "You are really too much sometimes."

"And you are a very aggravating child sometimes." He sighed. "Listen, just stick with the plan and continue to follow orders. This woman is very important for several reasons. Let us worry about them. You just continue to give us your feedback. We'll tell you what you need to know and when."

The phone went dead, so she put it in the seat next to her. It was not long before she was pulling into her apartment building. She grabbed her cell phone and her laptop. By habit, she looked around to make sure that no one was following her.

When she was sure it was safe, she quickly made her way to her apartment. It was on the ground floor, of course. She punched in the security code and opened the door. Her apartment was rather spacious. She sometimes thought that a family of four could live there without too many problems. It was sad that she had it all alone.

She quickly shook her head. She could not think thoughts like that, especially after meeting Andrea face to face. After seeing the pictures of her, she had already been quite attracted to the sandy blond before they had met. It had been hard to keep up her act while looking at her.

And it was sad. She had felt this instant chemistry between the two of them. But that was not a possibility. Even if she ever did sleep with her, it would be for the job. Her damn job, the one that her father had recruited her for, and he would not take no for an answer.

She shook her head at the thought. What was even more annoying was the fact that he was really her stepfather. She loved him like her own father, but this man did not love her like his daughter. In her heart, she knew he was only using her while he could.

Alicia made her way into the kitchen. She opened the refrigerator and took out a bottled water. It was all she drank. With the stress of her job and the stress her father had added, she long ago had developed an ulcer. She had to be very careful what she drank and ate. It made going undercover difficult sometimes.

Slowly, she made her way into the living room. She could not help but wonder why she had not heard back from Andrea. In her mind, she knew she had done just the right acting job to entice the woman. And yet, kept herself pulled back far enough. Was it all an act?

That was when the phone rang, making her focus again. She quickly answered it. "Hello?"

"Alicia?" The male voice practically squeaked out her name.

"Speaking."

"This is Adam from Freemont Investigations." He swallowed hard. "Miss Freemont has asked me to offer you the position if you're still interested."

A smile came across her face. "Of course I'm still interested. This is one great opportunity. When would she like me to come in?"

"Tomorrow if you're available." Again, his voice squeaked.

"Tell her I'll be there at nine." She hung up the phone. She thought, *First part of the mission accomplished, now on to phase two of the wonderful plan.*

Two men in gray business suits were having lunch in the back room of Chez Pierre. It was a very exclusive restaurant. Even though it was the busy lunch hour, they had the private dining room all to themselves as usual.

"Now, Henry," an African American man with graying temples and a gray mustache began. "Are you really certain that your daughter can be trusted? Look at what happened when we used her on the Exted case. Or have you forgotten what it cost us?"

Henry sat down his glass of wine. "Do you really think I could forget that costly debacle?" He shook his head emphatically and sighed. "Sometimes, I feel she is so capable of handling any situation. But then, she lets her feelings get in the way."

"It is quite frustrating." The man took a bite of his steak. "We could have her watched if you're not entirely sure that we can trust her. There is a lot at stake. Most people don't realize what goes on in this town. Hell, what goes on all over the entire world."

Henry nodded in agreement. "You're right. People are so blind to the things that happen every day. I wonder if they were to find out that what goes on in countries like Iraq, Iran, and other Middle Eastern countries aren't really about chemical warfare and terrorists what they would do. No. I believe people would be quite disturbed to learn the truth."

"That is where The Company comes in." He smiled. "If it weren't for us taking on the things of the night, who would? The US government won't do a damn thing but make it look like they're going to war. It is quite sad really."

"Listen, James. I know all of this. I know how important it is to our mission." Henry sighed. "I do feel that we can trust her. For now." He picked up his glass of wine again. "If we can succeed on this one, we can finally rid ourselves of that pesky Gina. That woman has given us trouble for the past twenty years. And I'm still not sure why."

"I have my own sources. I may know if you're interested, my friend." James smiled at his counterpart.

"You know that I am interested." His eyes grew bright with anticipation. "That damn vampire has vexed me for twenty years. She claims to be on the side of good. Do you know how many times she has messed with my plans?" He slammed down his glass.

"I figured you'd be eager to learn." He leaned in closer, even though they were alone. The words were whispered so that no one could hear.

"You're not serious." James only smiled and nodded. "Well, that makes things that much more interesting, now doesn't it? If we don't succeed, she may very well be her own undoing. That is a pleasant thought indeed."

"What are you doing, Ricky?" The dark-haired female vampire asked. Ricky was just outside the emergency room of Sparrow Hospital. "You better not be doing what I think you are."

Ricky quickly turned around, fear instantly on his face. He was barely five feet tall, had black hair with a gold stripe down the middle, and his fangs were showing and dripping with blood. "Gina?" He took several steps away as the body slipped to the ground. "Please don't kill me."

A laugh escaped from Gina. "I'm not going to kill you. Hurt, maybe." Gina shook her head. "You know that you are not supposed to do that. Not while you're working for me and not where you could be discovered."

"I-I j-just got so hungry, that's all." Ricky was now visibly shaking. "I c-couldn't wait till I-I got back to my lair. I'm s-sorry. I-it won't happen again. I p-promise."

Gina stood shaking her head. "How come I'm having trouble believing you? Could it be because this is the third time in two months that I've caught you red handed? And I do know about the other four people you killed."

"I-I." He stopped himself. He knew that Gina would know. She knew everything that went on in the city. She was like the master over it. It was her city. "I'm just so weak."

"I know you are." Gina shook her head. She always wondered what the vampire was thinking that had sired Ricky. He was nothing more than a little worm. "But that doesn't make it right, now does it." He stared at the pavement. "Let's get out of here before anyone sees us. We need to talk about how things are going, especially with this new group in town."

Both quickly headed down the sidewalk. They were headed toward a frequented demon restaurant. "I've heard other talk."

Gina raised her eyebrows. "Tell me what you've heard. Is it anything new concerning those that are out to get me?"

Ricky nodded. They were now only two blocks away from Max's Bar and Grill. Anyone unassuming would think it just a typical restaurant. That was until you ventured into the basement. "I heard that Mr. James was putting out feelers about you. He's trying to find out what you're up to. I think that they have something really big going down." He began squirming as they continued to walk.

"Tell me what you're holding back, Ricky. I'm not in the greatest mood tonight." She gave him the look. The one that would terrify an executioner. "I'm already a little irritated with you for your lack of control. You don't want that to lead me to becoming cranky, now do you?"

Ricky swallowed hard. His body was slightly shaking. "O-of course not." He put his right hand to his left cheek. He still had a burn mark from where she had held a cigarette lighter from a car to his cheek. Even though he healed quickly as a vampire, this time it had left a scar.

Gina stopped suddenly. They were only about thirty feet from Max's. "I've changed my mind about going to Max's. Finish telling me what you know. But quickly." She looked around them. "I think we're being followed. That damn Henry and James." She turned and glared at Ricky.

"This something, I think they're trying to involve Andrea in it." Ricky quickly took two steps away from her.

The female vampire's eyes widened. "You can't be serious. They're going to try and use her to get to me. Those bastards." She began pacing back and forth. "Well, that would definitely explain the feeling I had earlier. I was right. I bet that redhead is a plant or something." A growl came out of her throat. "I will not let them hurt her. She's been through enough in a lifetime. If she ever found out about her father, it would kill her. And that's probably what they're going to do."

"Do you want me to do something to help?" Ricky stood shaking in his shoes.

Gina kept pacing. Her mind was racing with all the things that were going on. "This is going to be a difficult situation. Get the newbies together. Tomorrow night at eight. We need to meet somewhere private."

"How about behind the mall? At that time of night, there is hardly anyone there." He smiled a small smile. "Besides, they wouldn't expect us to meet there."

Finally, Gina stopped her pacing. "It's rare, but sometimes you do prove yourself worthy if you'd just lay off the killing of people. Tell the newbies to watch it. Andrea is already getting suspicious. We don't need to give her any more reasons to go after us. Especially now that The Company is stepping up its effort to try and find me."

Ricky nodded his head. "Is that all? I'm still feeling a little peckish. I didn't drain that guy completely." He smiled as if expecting some type of gratitude.

"Well, that is something." Gina quickly came face to face with Ricky. "Just remember this, even leaving live ones brings up questions we don't want anyone finding out the answers to. So don't be feeding on humans anymore. Got it?" Gina smiled sweetly at the little vampire.

"Yes, Gina, I d-definitely got it." He took off running down the street.

Gina shook her head. "What I wouldn't do for better help." She looked around her. She could feel his presence. "I know you're out there, Henry. Maybe someday we'll go one on one. But not tonight. I have too many things to do." Her black hair bounced along her back she moved so quickly.

25

Andrea was tossing and turning in her bed. She really hated the nightmare. It was the same nightmare she had been having since she was eleven years old. She and her father were walking in the alleyway. The vampires showed up out of nowhere. They killed her father just like it had happened, nearly twenty years before. But unlike what happened back then, her friend Gina attacked and killed her, as well as the vampires.

She woke up screaming. Like she did every time she had the dream. Her eyes scanned the room. The little one room apartment had not changed. It was just as grimy looking as ever. Even in the darkness, she could see a roach crawling along the floor. She shivered as she saw it.

What was even more depressing was the fact that her bed was empty, as always. She sighed. It had been a long time since someone else had shared the double bed. But it was not necessarily because of lack of opportunity. Although there were not a whole lot of women available. Andrea had long ago learned not to trust anyone, with the exception of Gina. And Gina was a vampire. These dreams she kept having were telling her that she could not trust her, not anymore.

Andrea got out of bed. She walked over to the refrigerator. She took out the half gallon of milk. After taking one sip, she spit it back out. She looked at the expiration date. The milk was past two weeks of being good. She sighed as she went to the sink and dumped out the remaining contents.

Her dream again flashed in her mind. Gina had come to her rescue so many times. Why would she be dreaming that Gina was now out to get her? It made no sense whatsoever. In her short life, she had learned not to judge by looking at people. She knew of a muskrat demon that looked very much like a muskrat. But he was as sweet as a puppy and would not harm a fly.

And Gina was definitely always watching out for her. Why would she have these feelings to beware of the woman, granted a vampire, who had helped her out so many times in the past. Maybe her mind was just working overtime. After all, there appeared to be a new batch of vampires in town. And these ones definitely liked to sink their teeth into humans.

Suddenly, her mind flashed to the redhead. She shook her head trying to get Alicia's beautiful face out of her mind. The clock read 3 a.m. In just a few hours, she would be working very closely with the sexy woman.

This was not what she had wanted. She cursed herself for letting her libido talk her into hiring the woman. Granted, Alicia was over qualified for the position. And she was smart, funny, and sexy.

Again, Andrea shook her head. There was no way she could continue thinking that way and work with the woman. With some of the things going on with Gina, she needed somebody who was a computer expert. She only knew a little about the machines. Adam was quite good himself. But not like this woman appeared to be.

In addition, Alicia wanted to learn the business of being a private detective. It actually was not that difficult. Once you got some contacts, both on the force and on the streets, it was really quite simple getting the answers you wanted. Fortunately, she still had a couple connections to the cops because of her father and because of the six months she had been on the force. Some of them seemed a little leery of helping her though.

That was one of the biggest things that she wanted to know. The way things had gone down in that alleyway with those vampires made it sound like her father was into dirty dealings. Since she had been a private detective, she had yet to come up with the answers she had been looking for. It was almost like somebody was burying what had happened all those years ago.

Not the most pleasant of thoughts as Andrea got back into bed. But it was better than having her thoughts dwell on Alicia. Damn! So much for not thinking about her. What was it about this woman that was getting to her? Yeah, sexy, smart, sophisticated. Those were all the things that Andrea herself was not. Well, she was street smart, just not with the books.

Andrea looked at the clock. It clicked to 3:15. She knew she was going to be seeing the clock turn almost every minute. Her mind was working too much. But that was part of the reason that she was so good at her job and also why she was so often in trouble. A mind that never stopped working was both a curse and a gift. But mostly, it was a curse.

Adam had a smirk on his face as he watched Andrea yawning yet again. He often wondered what she did at night to come into the office so sleepy. But at the same time, he really did not want to know, either.

It was closing in on 9 a.m. and that meant their newest employee would be showing up soon. From what little he had seen of her, he really liked her. He was just hoping that this would not be like the last time.

Andrea had tried hiring a hacker, as she liked to call them, before. And it had been a woman as well. His boss had taken a liking to the girl right away and in more than just a friend sorta way. But she was straight. The relationship had gotten strained, and it was not long until they parted on not such good terms. He missed her sometimes.

But this Alicia was really different. There was just something about her. He had noticed the look that Andrea had given as Alicia left yesterday. He was no dummy. There was definitely a spark between the two.

Adam just hoped that the two would be able to get along. He was not sure about Alicia and how she felt. He definitely knew how his boss felt. She wore her heart on her shirt sleeve, as that old saying goes. Even though she tried acting tough, she was really easy to read once you got to know her well enough.

His thoughts were interrupted by the door opening. He looked up to see the redheaded woman. Alicia smiled at him. It took him a minute, but he finally found his voice. "Good morning, Miss Walker. Nice to see you again."

"Adam." She smiled and nodded. "Please call me Alicia. Is the boss in?"

He nodded. "She's expecting you. But make sure you call her Andrea. She hates being called anything else. Just knock before you go in. I think she has a project for you already."

"Cool." She started toward the door. She turned back to Adam. "And Adam?" He looked up at her. She smiled brightly. "I'm glad to be working with you." Before he could say anything, she was knocking on the door.

"Come in." Andrea was sitting on her desk with several files lying around. There were a few on the floor as well. "Hey, Alicia. Thanks for taking the job." She kept her sights on the hurricane that surrounded her.

"Looks like you've already been busy this morning." Alicia carefully made her way around the files on the floor. She sat on the opposite side of the desk. "Anything you need help on?"

Andrea finally looked up from the file she had been reading. "Always need help around here. No one ever seems to want to stick around for long. And I'll warn you now. It's not always a nine to five job." She picked up a file and handed it to Alicia. "This one isn't an actual paying client anymore, but I think there may be a connection to another one that is paying. Besides, I really hate loose ends."

Alicia opened the file. Inside were pictures of a dead man with puncture wounds on his neck. "Oh, my!" Her face paled a little at the sight.

"I'm so sorry." Andrea reached for the file, but Alicia kept a tight grip on it. "I forgot that the pictures of Mr. Claymore were in there. I should have warned you. Are you all right?"

"I've actually seen worse." Alicia shrugged at the look of surprise on the sandy blond's face. "I worked for the Police Department for a little while helping them organize their files. They also have some interesting files such as these."

"Still, it would have been nice to have a little heads up." Andrea took out another file. "There seems to be an epidemic of death by puncture wounds of the neck." She eyed her newest employee very carefully before she continued. "I probably should have asked you this yesterday." Alicia turned her attention from the file to her new boss. "Do you believe in the supernatural?"

Alicia shrugged. "What exactly is it that you're talking about when you say supernatural? Ghosts, demons. I mean, there are a lot of things that can be classified as supernatural."

"Well, you at least seem open to the possibility." She looked into the redhead's eyes. She was searching for a possible answer to her next question. "Do you believe that vampires are real?"

"I'd say by the looks of this they are." The redhead glanced at the notes that went along with the file. "Mrs. Claymore was told that it was a gang that was doing some type of ritual, that's why there were these punctures on his neck. What did the coroner's report say?"

"I'm not sure." Andrea shrugged. "Mrs. Claymore wasn't a paying client very long. And I haven't had a chance to get to the coroner's office to get a report. I have a friend down there that would kindly give us the information."

"That's not necessary." Alicia sat down in the chair in front of the desk. It brought her and Andrea very close. "If you'll allow me to have use of your computer and the internet, we'll have the information in a couple keystrokes."

"By all means." Andrea could feel her heart beating a little faster. Alicia's arm brushed against her leg. That was when she decided she needed a little distance between her and the sexy woman. "You didn't really answer my question." She began picking up some of the files and putting them together, all to avoid the closeness that was now between the two.

Alicia looked up at her. "You mean, about the vampires?" Andrea nodded. "Well, let's just say that I've had an experience with something and wasn't exactly sure what it was. It being a vampire makes as much sense as anything." She paused her typing. "Are you telling me that besides vampires, there are other things of the supernatural variety out there?" The computer beeped, and she began typing again.

Andrea again eyed her newest employee. She seemed to be taking this better than most would. Adam had passed out the first time he realized that Gina was a vampire. But then again, Adam was Adam. "Yeah, the way I like to say it, everything you ever were told wasn't real is. Everything you can imagine is probably real as well. That's the world I live in. Most people ignore the strange things of life and give it half plausible explanations."

"You mean like gangs doing rituals." Alicia smiled a small smile. "I guess I can understand people's reluctance to accept that certain things are real. If I hadn't had my own personal experience, I may think you were crazy as well." She hit a few more keys. "Got it." Andrea came to stand behind her. "Would have been faster if you had a faster connection."

"I'll have to look into that if and when I can afford it." She looked at what was showing on the screen. "There's no way in hell it could have happened like that. Knife wounds, my ass." Alicia looked up at her. "Sorry if the language offends. I'm like a sailor sometimes."

"That's not what I was surprised by. You understand what it says." Alicia pointed to all the medical terminology. "No offense intended, but it doesn't seem like you're into the big words."

"Hey, I can read the word *knife*." Andrea straightened a little at the perceived insult she had just received. "Besides, I was a cop." Alicia raised her eyebrows. "Only for six months, but still." Andrea shrugged. "I pick up things really easily, and once I learn them, it stays with me."

"Sorry didn't mean to offend you." Alicia chuckled. "I think we both have some preconceived ideas about each other." She turned back to the computer. "It's going to be interesting finding out about the real person behind the tough private detective's persona you've got going for you."

Andrea also let out a small laugh. "I guess you're right about the preconceived thing. You are a little more open minded than I thought you'd be. No offense, but computer experts are perceived as kinda stuffy and not so into things that aren't orderly and, of course, there is the supernatural."

"Well, I can dispel that myth right now. I like hanging out at Trippers and watching almost any sport. Except golf. Never could understand that one." Alicia was still typing away at the keyboard. "You like sports?"

Alicia nodded in response, never taking her eyes off the computer screen.

"Well, that is a pleasant surprise. Maybe we could go together sometime. I'll warn you, I'm a big U of M fan myself."

"Wrong territory, at least for where we're at right now." Alicia looked up from the computer. "But I'm with you a hundred percent. Go Wolverines." The computer beeped at her again. "Look at this." She pointed to the screen. On it was a list of fifteen people over the last week that had either died of neck punctures or at least had to receive treatment from one of the various local hospitals.

Andrea came and took a look. "Now that's what I call a definite vampire indicator. Damn!"

Alicia looked up, a little startled. "What's wrong, other than a lot of people getting hurt?"

"That's just it." Andrea began pacing back and forth. "I was kinda told that there was a new vampire pack in town." She found Alicia staring at her when she looked up. "I didn't do anything 'cause my source is known to be a drunk. I can only believe half of what he tells me. Hell, he usually works for whiskey."

"You actually pay for information by giving a wino booze?" Alicia looked really surprised.

"I've tried giving him money. Hell, I've tried giving him food." She sighed. "He won't talk unless it is some type of booze. I shouldn't, but sometimes his information is invaluable. Like this would have been if I would have listened to him."

"Sorry." Alicia could see the hurt look on Andrea's face. "Didn't mean to sound so judgmental. I'm still new to this whole private detective thing. I'm sure there are a lot of little things that don't sound good to the average person but get the job done. Especially for good reasons."

"Thanks for that. And I am doing this for a good reason." Andrea started to pace again. "The last time a group of vampires made their way to Lansing, the end toll was three hundred victims in two months. Fortunately, only fifty of them resulted in deaths. Still, that's a large number. And we now know of at least three confirmed deaths and at least a dozen more injuries. I'm so not liking this. I may have to…"

Alicia looked up from the computer. She noticed that Andrea had stopped pacing. It was as if Andrea were really studying her, trying to tell if she could trust her or not. Which, she really should not. If only Andrea knew that she was basically a double agent, she would not trust her at all.

"You may have to what?" Alicia hated asking. But it was part of the job. She needed to get Andrea to trust her. Whether she liked to trick this woman or not.

"Well," Andrea hesitated still. She was not sure if she could trust her with the knowledge that Gina was out there and helping fight the evil that existed. "Let's just say I have a special friend. And this friend is better equipped to deal with vampires and the supernatural. Especially if they are in a group like I think they are. From what we've seen, this group looks pretty damn large."

"I agree." She stood up from the desk. "You don't have to tell me about everything that goes on in the office, not yet anyway. You don't know that much about me, and I don't know that much about you. It's gonna take time before we can truly trust each other. And that's the way it should be."

Andrea smiled. "Thanks for understanding. I do want to say a little more about the whole demon thing. Just to let you know, demons and vampires are just like humans in that it isn't always clear if they're evil or good. Just because they are different doesn't mean that they are automatically evil."

Alicia raised her eyebrows. "Since this whole demon thing is all new to me, I'll take your word for it. Is there anything I can do to protect myself from those that don't wear the white hats?"

Andrea burst out laughing. "Sorry. It's just the white hat thing. It's an interesting way of putting it. As far as the protection thing, it's really standard stuff like you see in the movies and on television. Vampires really don't like garlic and crucifixes. Holy water, sunlight, decapitation, fire, and wooden stake through the heart are the best ways to kill them. With each demon, it varies. But usually decapitation or a sharp object to the heart are your best bets."

"Interesting. Just like in the movies." She shrugged. "Who knew?" She smiled. "So is there anything else you need my computer skills for?"

Andrea looked at her. "You really are eager to learn all about this, aren't you?"

"Let's just say I've lived a sheltered life. I've been wanting to find something a little more stimulating." She eyed her boss before continuing. "I think I've found it working with you."

Andrea swallowed hard as she felt her heart skip a couple beats. The woman seemed to be coming on to her again. No. It was just all this information that had the woman so stimulated. It could not be her. It was never her.

"I've got to compile a couple things. A couple of these cases are definitely related by the vampire thing. That much is obvious. Maybe, after I get them sorted, you can help me set up a database, and we can cross reference them. Really see where the connections are if there are any."

"Sounds like a plan." Alicia looked at her watch. It was already closing in on noon. "If you won't need me for a little while, I may just go grab some lunch. Unless, of course, you'd like to join me. Trippers isn't that far. And they have a great fajita. You game?"

Andrea's cheeks reddened a little. "That's all right. I still have a lot of work to do. Besides, I brought my lunch today. Maybe next time."

"Then it's a date. See you in a couple hours, boss." Alicia shot out the door before Andrea could say anything.

Again, Andrea swallowed hard. That was just an expression, right? *Date* meaning nothing more than two people at the same place at the same time. The woman was a real mystery. If Andrea read her right, she was coming on to her every chance she got. That was starting to make her just a little suspicious. Nobody usually came on to her. And what exactly was this encounter that had her instantly believing that vampires were real.

She sighed a big sigh and shook her head to try and clear it. With all these people either dead or hurt by these vampire attacks, she needed her mind at full capacity. And she would need to talk to Gina. That was it. That was just the thing to clear her mind. She needed to talk to her best friend.

Alicia slowly pulled into the parking lot. She hated coming to this fancy place. But Chez Pierre was the only place her father would meet her. It was somehow his safe haven. She still did not understand that.

The maitre'd glanced at her as she headed to the private dining room. He knew better then to stop her. She was definitely expected. And by the people he feared most in the world.

She opened the door. The man she called father, known as Henry to his compatriots, sat eating a steak dinner and looking over his notes. His dusty blonde hair was a little out of place which was very unusual for him.

He looked up and pointed to the chair farthest from him. "Alicia." She sat down in the assigned chair. "And how goes it on your first day of your new job?"

"Don't you mean assignment?" She smiled at the scowl she received. "Everything seems to be going along just fine. I'm making progress on both the business and personal front. She even mentioned a special friend that she has."

His eyes quickly found hers. A little smile played at the corners of his mouth. "If this is who we are after, this is very good indeed." He leaned back in his chair. "Are you certain that this is a special friend she is talking about? And are you really sure that she is…"

"Falling for my feminine charms?" The redhead watched as her father's face turned a nice shade of red. She caught herself before she smiled again. "I'm sure on that account. I told her that she didn't have to confide anything to me that she didn't want to. Not yet. Too new into the relationship and all that. Who is this special friend, and what is so special about her that you are after her?"

"That information is classified. And you are not quite at the rank for that information." He stood and began pacing. "Listen, Alicia my dear, what is with all the questions? You know that The Company works best with those higher ups giving the orders and those lower following them without asking any questions. There are those that are beginning to question your loyalties. And you know what that would mean."

"And since when do you not share information with me?" She shook her head. "You've always told me everything about my assignments. All of a sudden, you're not sharing what I consider vital information. If I knew what was up with this special friend, like her name, I might be able to better track Andrea's coming and goings. And what the hell do I care about some stuffed shirts questioning my loyalty. That James is an asshole. Has been since the minute he got promoted over you."

Henry shook his head. "Please. It's only in your best interest if you follow orders and not make a fuss. We may not be able to replace you now. Even though it's only been one day, it seems that you are already in deep with this Andrea." Alicia blushed at the mention of her boss' name. He could not help but notice. "Are you falling for this woman? You remember what happened on the Exted case."

Alicia sighed heavily. "I remember very well. I also remember my training. I would be very stupid to allow myself to have any feelings toward this woman, whether they were only friendship or more serious. I've been doing this for a long time. You are the one that trained me, remember."

"How could I forget?" He softly smiled to himself. "You were stubborn as ever. You wanted to do things your own way back then as well. You've never really been one to follow the rules, now have you? And that's what just may cost us this current project. You have got to learn to follow the rules." They sat in silence for a few minutes. "Would you care for something to eat?"

She looked up at him. The thought that she was betraying her boss played in her mind. She was not supposed to think like this. It was only an assignment after all. It should not matter that the woman could get hurt. "Suddenly, I'm really not all that hungry."

Andrea held her nose as she made her way through the sewer. She probably should have called first, but she needed to see her friend as soon as possible. Almost every day at this time, Gina was watching the local news and sharpening her swords or making new wooden stakes.

She could see the light coming from Gina's lair. That meant that she was probably there. That was a good thing. As attracted as she had become to her newest employee, there was a vibe that she was not sharing everything. And in this line of business, that got people hurt.

Before she could get to the entrance, she heard voices. One of them was definitely Gina's. She was not sure, but she thought the other belonged to a vampire named Ricky. He was a smarmy little guy. What in the world was Gina doing talking to that creep? It did not make any sense.

"Has the meeting been set up?" Gina's voice came from the entrance to her lair.

The creepy male's voice responded. "At eight, just behind the Lansing Mall, just as you requested. All the newbies are gonna be there. It seems your reputation has preceded you. They are more than just a little terrified of you."

"As they should be." Andrea heard Gina let out a low growl. "They really are making a mess out of this whole situation. They were supposed to lay low and wait for the right time. It may be weeks now before we can go through with the plan. And I have The Company breathing down my neck."

"Is there anything you wish me to do?" Ricky sounded eager to please. "If there is, I'd be happy to do it for you, Gina."

"I know you would." Andrea could hear her begin to pace. "Right now, I'm afraid for Andrea. She is being set up by this redhead. I don't know for sure, but every fiber in my being tells me that she cannot be trusted. And then there is that matter with her father."

"I assure you that has been taken care of." Gina again growled low in her throat. "I know I've said this before, but I've taken care of all those that could possibly tell what really happened before the incident."

"You had better." There was a silence for a moment. "Can you smell that?"

"I wasn't breathing." He took a careful breath. "Oh, besides the noxious fumes. I think I smell a human."

"So do I." Gina began walking toward the entrance. "With the smell of the sewer, I can't quite make out whose scent. Let's find out, shall we." She made her way out of the lair with Ricky following close behind. They walked several paces. "Forget, it. The human has gone topside. I'm wondering who that was."

On the topside, Andrea was standing, tears forming in her eyes. This was all so unreal. She was not sure if she could trust her new employee. And now she was not sure if she could trust her friend anymore. Why was Gina in leagues with these new vampires that were definitely into biting humans? Were they good vampires who just lost control?

She shivered at the thought. She had seen Gina lose control only once in the almost twenty years she had known her. It was enough to know that if Gina could lose control, then any vampire could from time to time. But that many attacks in not many days, that just did not make sense.

None of this was making sense at the moment. Andrea quickly made it to her beat up car. It rattled, but it started. First she would go home and wash the smell of the damn sewers off herself. She would then start finding out if she really could trust her newest employee. And she would be going to the mall later tonight, possibly to catch an old friend red handed.

Alicia kept driving in circles. She knew that she should go back to the office as quickly as possibly. But she just could not face Andrea. What was going on between the two of them? They had not even really known each other a day, yet there seemed to be this connection.

They were different, yet they seemed to be the same. She was getting so tired of fighting the war that she was and not getting the least bit of recognition by her peers. At least Andrea had appreciated what little she had done so far.

There was only one person in the world she could talk to at this point. The only one that knew what she did for a living and how easily and quickly she fell for a good woman.

She headed the car to the north. It would be another half an hour before she got to her mother's house, but it would be worth it if she could clear things up like she always seemed to. Alicia did not want to get in over her head. After all, not only was she falling for this new woman in her life, she was also starting to question whether her stepfather and The Company were right.

Maybe Andrea was the one that was right. After all, it sounded like she had grown up in the demon world. Alicia was still new to it. Her stepfather had only trained her three years ago. She had been bored with the computer thing. Even though every company in the United States wanted her to work for them, it just did not feel right.

That was when her stepfather had talked her into joining his organization. It had been around since the early nineteen hundreds. Many men had gone to war, as he liked to call it, over the years. It was not until the last ten years that women were now allowed to join the organization, at least as a field operative like herself. The funny thing was that it had a front as a charitable organization. They even accepted donations.

With all these conflicting emotions, she was not sure any more if she had made the right choice. Even in the beginning, she had not liked following orders. She was much more of a doer than a follower. Sitting around waiting for orders was not her idea of a good time. In addition, she did not like the fact that she was supposed to obey without question.

And now, she had met the most interesting woman she had ever met. It kept coming back to her new boss. Every thought she had, it kept her coming back to the same person. Almost everything she had said was true. She was not just trying to get this woman to like her because it was the job. She knew in her heart she wanted this woman in every possible way.

The time flew by because her mind was so conflicted. She was now pulling into her mother's house. Her stepfather had left her mother a year ago. Part of the reason he had left was because her mother was not happy that he had recruited her for The Company.

The back door opened before she could even put the car in park. The short brunette woman with graying hair waved and smiled at her daughter. Alicia slowly got out of the car. Her mother was a very special woman. If anyone could figure this all out, it had to be her.

"Sweetie, what a pleasant surprise." Her mother held the door open for her. "But by the look on your face, you've come because your life has become too complicated again. The last time you had the look was when you had so much fun on that one case."

Alicia smiled. "You know me all too well." She sighed heavily and followed her mother into the living room. Both sat on the couch and faced each other. "I should be at my new job right now, but things have kinda gotten complicated. And it hasn't even been one day yet."

Her mother shook her head. "Your life has been complicated since you took that job. I still say that Henry should not have pushed you so hard." Alicia began to interrupt. Her mother held up a hand. "I know you are head strong and only do what you want. But if he hadn't enticed you in the first place, you never would have accepted the job."

Alicia shrugged. "Maybe. Maybe I would have come to him. I knew what his job was like. To me, it was a lot more exciting than what I was doing." She shook her head. "What's done is done. Once you're in, it's up to your superiors to kick you out. I can't simply quit. And if they feel that I've somehow sabotaged any of my assignments, they would find a way to put me in jail. They already tried that once."

Her mother nodded. "I remember. I had to beg with Henry just to speak on your behalf. He should have done that on his own." She looked at her daughter. "But the job is not what's really getting to you. I can tell. There is someone special in your life, isn't there?"

"Mom!" Alicia's cheeks began to redden. She sighed heavily before she answered. "You do know me so well. And as we've already established, it's complicated. She's a part of the assignment."

"Oh, dear." Her mother chuckled softly. "Is it like the last time when you found yourself attracted to that woman that turned out to be a vampire. And tried to kill you."

Alicia shook her head. "I definitely know that she's not a vampire. But…"

"But," her mother continued to gently push.

"But she believes that vampires can choose to be good." She shrugged. "She also believes that demons can be good as well. That they have some choice in the matter."

"You don't believe like she does."

"I'm not sure." Her gaze fell to her lap. "I've only come across vampires that were evil. Or at least told were evil by the higher ups. If there are good vampires out there, did I kill things that were actually innocents?"

"That would be a possibility if there are good vampires." Her mother's soothing voice continued. "Let me ask you a question, and please answer from your heart, not your head. Who do you trust? This new woman in your life or do you trust your stepfather and The Company?"

Alicia at first giggled. But then she thought long about what her mother had just asked. Her stepfather and The Company always told her to just do as she was told. She was expected to do whatever she was told. Even when every fiber told her to question them, she had followed orders blindly.

But Andrea was different. She had asked if she believed in the supernatural. She gave her proof and let her decide for herself. Andrea was not even trying to force her to believe that there were good and bad vampires. The choice was Alicia's to decide. It had been so long since somebody let her decide.

After what seemed like an eternity, Alicia finally answered her mother. "I think that Andrea is the one that I would have to trust. Both my gut instincts and my heart are telling me to trust this woman completely. I've never felt this way about anyone before. And I've only known her for about a day and a half. Is it possible that there is such a thing as love at first sight?"

"I believe it was love at first sight with your father." Her mother blushed at the memories that it brought up.

"You can't be serious." Alicia looked her mother in the eyes. "You and Henry in love at first sight?"

"Not Henry, your real father." Her mother chuckled softly.

"Oh." Alicia smiled. "Tell me about your first meeting. Maybe I can figure if I feel the same thing."

"Well," her mother leaned back into the soft couch. Her smile grew as she began remembering. "We were at our senior prom together. Both of us had dates. It turned out his best friend, my date, was his date's cousin. The four of us spent most of the night together. By the end of the night, your father is the one that took me home."

"Mother. You dumped your date to be with Daddy?" Alicia could not help but laugh. "So I'm guessing there was major sparkage between the two of you."

"Sparkage?" Her mother nodded as she got it. "Well, yes. A whole lot of sparkage. We danced the last dance before he took me home. My parents were still up. He offered to come in and meet them even though he wasn't the date I had left with. Your grandfather simply adored him."

"So not only was there sparkage, he met the parents on the first date." Alicia smiled. "Were you guys able to keep dating?"

"Until he left for college. Even then, we wrote every day to each other." She had little tears in the corner of her eyes. "By the end of his freshman year, he said he couldn't stand being without me. We were married that summer. It was a struggle, but we managed to survive. Until the car accident."

"I'm sorry, Mom. I shouldn't have asked you to tell me about it." She got up and gave her mother a hug. "You still love him very much, don't you?" Her mother only smiled in response. "I'm not so sure I could say our initial meeting was quite that romantic. In fact, Andrea tried to avoid me like the plague."

"Oh, and why would she want to avoid a beautiful woman like you?" She looked up at her daughter who was now standing in front of her. "She is gay, isn't she?"

"Definitely." She shrugged. "Maybe she's had a couple of bad experiences or something. Maybe she's your one night stand kind of girl. Or there is the possibility that she simply doesn't want an office romance. Maybe she suspects I'm there to spy on her. The possibilities are overwhelming."

"Listen. We've talked for a little while now." Her mother stood and hugged her. "I've listened to everything you've said. You came to me for advice, so here it is. Follow your heart. And forget what Henry has to say. I've learned that he is really just a pompous windbag. You are smarter than he is."

"Thanks, Mom." Alicia gave her another hug. "As always, you've come through for me again. I think I know what I'm going to do. Still, not a hundred percent sure though."

"I am."

Alicia looked at her mother quizzically.

"Bring the girl home to meet your mother."

Henry stared out the window of his office. It was on the fourteenth floor overlooking the Lansing Community College campus. He could see the hustle of the many college students. As always, his thoughts turned toward his son.

Fredrick was his pride and joy. Or had been until he got caught up in that gang of vampires. It was one of the reasons that Henry was now such a firm believer in the rules and regulations of The Company.

If his son had listened to him, he would still be alive today. But Gina took care of him very easily. Henry still had trouble believing what the vampire bitch had to say. Even though his son was turned, there was no way that he would have chosen evil. Even though The Company said that all vampires were evil, he knew in his heart that

43

just was not true. He had come across other vampires that were good as well.

The phone rang, interrupting his thoughts. He quickly made his way over to his desk. "Hello?"

"Henry, it's your ex, Eleanor." The female voice was full of annoyance. "How can you still be coming down so hard on our daughter? Hasn't she proven her loyalty?"

"She's your daughter or have you forgotten what you said to me before I left?" He sat down in his chair. "You didn't want your daughter joining my business. Yet if Fredrick were still alive, I'm sure you would have no trouble letting him join."

"Henry, how can you say that?" Eleanor sighed heavily. "I always tried to treat the children the same. Do you think I would have wanted him in the same danger as Alicia? Do you think it's easy that he's gone? It's been twenty years but seems longer."

"I'm surprised you know how long it has been. I thought you'd be too busy with your daughter to even give my son a second thought." He leaned back in his chair. His left hand came to his right temple. "You're giving me a headache."

"Well, that's nothing new, now is it?" She again sighed. "Honestly, Henry, I only called to ask that you don't push her so hard. You know that she already has health issues. Sometimes I think you're trying to kill her so that you won't be the only one that lost a child."

"You can be such a bitch." Henry slammed the phone down. He stood up and began pacing. The thought that Alicia had gone running to her mother did not bode well. It either meant that she was having trouble with following orders as always or she was really falling for this woman. Either way, it would mean trouble.

"Damn!" He stopped pacing and walked back over to his desk and picked up the phone. After dialing a number, he waited for an answer. "James, I'm afraid we have a slight problem. You might just want to start following Alicia after all. Her head may not totally be in the game."

Andrea was trying to concentrate on the files she had laid around her. It was nearing seven. She was going to the mall at eight to find out what Gina was up to and was just trying to kill time. There still seemed to be a connection between some of the cases. It just was not yet clicking. She was also wondering where the hell that Alicia had run off to. Lunch did not take eight hours. Hell, she hardly ate at all herself.

Maybe there had been a family emergency. Maybe she was trying to do something on her own. Or, more likely, maybe she was conspiring behind her back.

The feeling she got at the thought of the woman betraying her disturbed her in many ways. She had been afraid of hiring a woman for this very reason. She often let herself fall for the wrong woman. And when she did, she fell hard. The last time had been a real disaster. Andrea liked the redhead way too much to think these bad thoughts about her. But what else was she supposed to think? The woman was definitely hiding something. That much was crystal clear. Unfortunately, nothing else was at this point.

Her thoughts were interrupted by a knock on the door. "Who is it?" she asked as she started picking up one of the piles.

"It's Alicia. Can I come in?" The voice sounded strained and nervous. That was very unusual for the self confident woman that Andrea had met yesterday.

Andrea's head shot up. "I'm just going through more files. Come in." She tried to read the expression on the other woman's face as she walked in. For the moment, it was purely blank. She was unreadable. "I sure could have used you earlier. That database would have come in handy." She was trying to keep the conversation toward neutral things. The need to keep the fact that she had doubts about the other woman a secret was great.

Alicia squatted down next to her boss. "Do you have time for a long talk?"

Andrea gathered a few of the files and stood up. Alicia did as well. Andrea looked at her watch and sighed. "Not really. I have a meeting at eight. And it's across town. I'm probably going to have to get going now."

"Oh." Alicia's voice got really sad and distant. "It can wait, but it is really important that we talk and before too long. I really need to tell you something."

Andrea looked at her quizzically. "Is there something wrong? Are you not happy working with me 'cause it's hardly been one day, even though I know I'm not the easiest person to get along with most of the time."

"No, that's definitely not it. I've really enjoyed working with you so far." She said it so quickly that Andrea almost did not understand. Alicia took a deep breath before she continued. "I want to talk to you tonight if you don't mind. I don't care how late it is, but I feel that it can't wait much longer. You need to hear what I have to say." Her eyes also got very sad and distant.

Andrea put a hand on the red head's shoulder. She felt an instant sensation. It was unlike any feeling she had ever felt before. "Damn! This sounds really serious." She looked at her watch. "If this meeting wasn't crucial, I'd stay and talk. I really want to hear what you have to say. But I promise that this is imperative to the whole recent events."

"You mean the vampire attacks?"

"Yeah. It feels like the two things are very connected." She looked deep into the redhead's eyes. "I'm just not sure yet. When I find out, I'll tell you what's what." She pulled the red head a little closer. "If you don't mind, we could meet later at one of our places. You said you didn't mind the lateness. This could take a little while."

Alicia smiled. Her whole body was beginning to tingle at the touch of Andrea's hands and their closeness. "I'd really like that. Shall we meet at my place? It's right on Kalamazoo."

"I know where you live." Andrea smiled at the surprised look on Alicia's face. "I know some things about you. But you are still a mystery. And I love mysteries." Andrea was shocked by her own words. She was never this brazen when it came with flirting with another woman. She was usually a little more subtle. Subtle. Hell, she never made the first move with other women.

"I love a good mystery as well." Alicia put her hand on Andrea's hip. There were a number of sensations going to Andrea's brain, all of them very pleasurable. "You are full of mysteries as well." Their heads slowly moved toward each other. Just as their lips were about to touch, Alicia whispered, "Unfortunately, don't you have to get going?" Andrea looked more than a little disappointed. "We can finish our little talk and more later. See you after your meeting." Slowly, Alicia walked toward the door. She turned and half smiled at the sandy blonde. A little wave and she disappeared out the door.

Andrea turned and stared a moment after the beautiful woman. Alicia was definitely interested in her which made her heart do a little dance. But she was also a mystery. There were a lot of unresolved questions surrounding her. But first, there was the mystery with Gina. Andrea was determined to find out what was beneath the surface of both women.

The mall parking lot was nearly empty. Gina stood in front of a green van, surveying the surrounding area. She knew that Henry was determined more than ever to bring her down. All she really wanted to do was good. But sometimes, you had to cross the line to achieve that.

Headlights flashed twice as another van, only blue, pulled into the parking lot. It finally parked next to her. Ricky was the first out of the van. He was followed by a group of eighteen vampires.

Gina's eyes widened a little at the number. From what Ricky had told her, the group only consisted of two males and eight females. This group had ten males and eight females.

Again, Gina's eyes scanned the parking lot. She listened with her better than human hearing. There seemed to be nothing. But looks could very well be deceiving. She had been fooled one too many times.

A tall blonde male vampire stuck out his hand. "So you're the big queen of these parts. It's so nice to meet you."

Gina simply glared at the hand she was offered until he pulled it back. "I'm hoping I can say the same about you and your friends. But it hasn't started out that way, now has it?"

The blonde took two steps back. "Yeah, well, we're not used to having to answer to anybody. And we don't always feed on humans like that, but you gotta admit. Humans just taste so much better then animal blood."

A growl came out of Gina's throat. "I know very well that fact. But if you are serious about really choosing to help others, you will learn to restrain yourselves from now on. Do we understand each other?"

"Sure, sure." The blonde kept his eyes on Gina. He was simply terrified. The group standing behind him refused to even make eye contact with her. She simply exuded a power that none of them had ever felt before. It was terrifying.

"I told you these guys would understand." Ricky came and stood next to Gina. "When I tell you something, you can always believe it."

Gina rolled her eyes. "Please. I know you better than that, Ricky. You only fall in line when you think I'll find out what you're up to. Just to let you all know, I have eyes and ears everywhere, so watch your step."

"It's cool." The blonde pointed to the group standing behind him. "We're down with anything you say, girl."

A heavy sigh escaped Gina. She could tell that these guys were not the brightest bulbs on the ole Christmas tree. "Well, that's very good. Listen carefully to the plan. The Company is getting closer and closer to finding out where I am. If that happens, they'll kill me. That may sound good to you, but then who will protect your sorry asses when they come for you. Once I'm out of the way, you know they'll be gunning for you."

"That's why this is your town."

Gina's look told Ricky to shut up.

"I don't like having to kill humans, but we may just have to." She looked around again. It was as if she could sense somebody familiar. "But from what I can gather, James and Henry are the two that are gunning for me. They know I know all of their dark secrets. The rest of The Company would rather ignore my existence. And with Henry, it's personal. He won't stop at anything to get his hands on me."

"So what exactly do you want us to do?" the tall blonde asked. His voice did not hide the fear he felt.

"It's simple. I have a list of where certain operatives live. We begin kidnaping, not killing, them." She turned to Ricky. "Are the warehouses still available?"

"Yeah." He thought for a moment. "I can get them stocked with water and other essentials tonight."

"You're thinking smart again. It's scary." She turned back to the rest of the vampires. "Start by gathering as many as you can tonight. I want to set up a meeting between me and Henry. I figure if we gather enough of these operatives, they'll be forced to talk with me. Then I can hopefully put an end to this damn conflict that has been going on for the last twenty years."

A black-haired female stepped forward. "Can I ask what we're going to do if this doesn't work?"

"Unless I can think of something else, we'll take out The Company." Gina growled low in her throat. "Permanently."

Andrea gasped at the last thing that Gina said. She pulled the headphones off her head and quickly took care of the listening device she had been using. She was suddenly getting a sick to her stomach feeling.

Gina was actually planning on possibly killing humans. She had never even thought that Gina would do such a thing. Once, when she had lost control, she had bitten a man. But she had stopped herself before she had killed him.

There was another thing that was bothering her. Who was this damn The Company? She had never heard of the organization. Apparently, they were after Gina and other vampires.

Her head began hurting as she pulled out of the theater parking lot. It sat across from the mall and had made a perfect place for her to hide out and spy on her friend. She was not sure where to go. It felt like Gina had just betrayed her in the biggest way possible. She reached into her pocket and found the paper with Alicia's address on it.

Could she trust this woman? That was the next question. It did not appear that she could trust her best friend anymore, at least not to tell her what was going on.

She had fought along side Gina for many years now. For her not to trust her with this big time information hurt a lot. And it left her with no one to trust.

Again, the address was in her hand. What would it hurt to go and listen to what the woman had to say. Maybe she was just a woman coming on to her. Maybe she was trying to find someone like she had always been.

Her mind drifted back to their earlier encounter as she headed toward Kalamazoo Street. The feeling she had gotten the moment her hand had touched Alicia's shoulder was one she had never gotten before. It was like it was on fire. It had been difficult to leave and yet impossible to move.

It had been a similar feeling when Alicia had put her hand on her hip. There was definitely a heat coming from her hand. It was not a natural heat. It was the heat of want and passion.

And, of course, her heart had nearly stopped beating, and she had forgotten to breathe as their lips nearly touched. They had been so close and yet so far apart. She so wanted to feel the touch of the woman's lips on hers.

But Andrea would have to use self control. As much as she wanted to simply throw that woman on a bed and show her who really was boss, she knew that they had to talk. Talking was the thing that the two of them needed to do. Maybe then she could get the answers she was looking for and somebody she could actually trust.

It was now two in the morning. Alicia paced back and forth in her apartment. It was not looking like Andrea was coming. Her meeting might have been longer than anticipated, but she should have been here by now.

Her mind was not only on one thing. Telling Andrea the truth, that was what she needed to do. This woman had been understanding so far. She did not want to blow a possible relationship with her. Screw what her stepfather said. The Company could also go screw themselves as well. She did not care anymore.

She was startled by a knock on her door. Quickly, she went over to the door. On the other side of the peep hole was Andrea. And the woman was not looking too good.

Quickly, she removed the chain. "Come in." She stood back and let her enter. Alicia closed the door and put the chain back in place. She also turned on her security alarm.

Andrea was standing in the middle of the room. Her eyes kept darting around. "Nice place you got here. Don't know how you're going to keep it on what I'm paying you."

Alicia came over and took both the other woman's hands in her own. "What's wrong? And don't tell me nothing. I can tell by the look on your face."

"Me?" Andrea removed her hands even though the contact was very comforting. But it was also very stimulating. She needed a clear mind to think right now. "Just wasn't the best of news from my meeting, that's all."

"Come and sit down." Alicia practically dragged Andrea to the couch in the living room. She sat next to her. "What happened or don't you want to talk about it?"

"I'm not sure I can, not yet anyway." Alicia sat back a little at the tone of Andrea's voice. "It seems that there is no one I can trust anymore besides Adam. And let's face it, Adam really doesn't count."

"You can trust me." Again, Alicia tried taking Andrea's hand in her own. But Andrea pulled hers away. "Please don't pull away from me. I don't think I have anyone left to trust, either. Except for my mom. And that really doesn't count, not in the way we are talking about."

Andrea finally turned and looked at the redhead. "You're not sure if you can trust anyone, either?" She stared at her for a moment. "But you think you can trust me? Why?"

Alicia laughed softly. "Because I think I already know you. Better than you want to admit."

"There was only one person that really knew me, and she's now doing things I never would have thought she would." Her stare became even more intense. "I know you're not just simply a hacker. I know that you specifically came to work for me. I think it was because of my friend. I have to know something. Who is The Company, and how do you fit into all this?"

Alicia smiled. "I should have known you would be smart enough to figure things out." She moved closer. "The Company is an organization, not government, just a bunch of business suits that got together in the early nineteen hundreds. It all started when one man's daughter was raped and killed by a pack of men. He found out that they were vampires."

"So that's how you knew about vampires." Andrea shook her head. "So this man, did he set this group up to act as some kind of vigilantes against vampires?"

"You guessed it." She sighed. "More and more men decided to join forces. They began training operatives to fight the walking dead. Their numbers grew larger. But the vampires kept coming. So they expanded. The Company is now a world wide organization. One of its offices is right here in Lansing. That's the one I work out of."

"You work for these guys?" Andrea shook her head. "I'm having trouble believing that you would just simply follow along with these stuffy old men. You seem smarter than that."

"Thanks. But once you are recruited, you're in for life until a higher up says differently." She frowned. "And if it appeared that I was sabotaging any of my missions, they would see I ended up in jail."

"Have you ever been in jail like it says on your resume?"

Alicia shook her head. "Just part of the cover. I have worked for those companies though. I've been an operative for three years now. My stepfather recruited me."

"Wow." Andrea stood up and began pacing. "What exactly is it that made me so damn important? I know it's not my good looks. Who or what do I know that is so important to invade my life like this?"

"Your looks alone would have attracted me." Andrea stopped pacing at the comment and looked at her. "But I believe it's your special friend. I don't know anything about her, not even her name. I was just told to get in good with you so that you might lead me to her."

"Get in good?" Now there was an anger flashing in Andrea's eyes. "That's what this is all about, isn't it? You can tell me you were attracted to my looks, but I won't buy it. I'm nothing special. I'm just an ordinary woman. You were just using me."

"I'll be honest." Alicia stood and was now face to face with Andrea. "The first day I was there, all that flirting. It was just to get in with you to make sure I got the job." She stepped even closer. "But things changed quickly. I couldn't stop thinking about you. My mind keeps focusing on you. Why the hell do you think I'm telling you all I know about what's going on?"

"Are you really? Or is this just some sympathy thing?" Andrea also stepped closer. "Are you trying to turn me on so that I will forget the real reason that I'm here? And that's to find out exactly what you know and if I can trust you." Their lips met suddenly. Both women gasped at the intensity that they felt. Finally, Andrea pulled away. "God, I so want to trust you. I need to trust you."

Alicia put her hand on Andrea's face. "You can. I'm not about to lie to you anymore. I think we both know that. There is too much of a connection, now. I think…"

Her words were cut off by an annoying whine. "What the hell is that?"

Alicia pulled Andrea closer to her. "We've got trouble. That's the alarm."

James paced back and forth in the dark alley. He really did not like meeting like this, but it was one of the few ways that the damn vampire would agree to meet with him.

A sound made him turn around in his tracks. "Who's there?" His voice echoed in the empty alleyway. He glanced at his watch, seeing that it was now nearing three, he really wondered where the vampire was. The meeting was supposed to have taken place an hour ago.

"Been waiting long?" Ricky stepped out of the shadows and into the dim light. "Sorry. I had to keep Miss Gina happy."

James nodded his head and made his way toward the vampire. "I understand. We both have our reasons to keep her happy. Are there any news on the front?"

"You mean the front that says that you and Gina had some dirty dealings twenty years ago." Ricky shrugged. "And that you and she are the reason that her best friend's father is dead?" He smiled at the look the man gave him. "Let's just say I now know the part that both of you had in all of that."

"This is sounding like you want to threaten me." James straightened himself. "Or do you mean to try and blackmail me? Either way, you'd best be careful what you're doing. I have a lot of connections. You could easily be dust blowing in the wind, pal."

"I'm not your pal." Ricky started pacing back and forth. "And believe me when I say you and your friends don't scare me. Not half as much as Gina. She's the one that I don't want finding out about our little arrangement."

"But she would be grateful that you got rid of all the reminders of her past discretions." James smiled as he watched Ricky pacing like a caged animal. "You've helped her hide the fact that she took innocent lives just to make a little money."

Ricky stopped pacing. He turned quickly to face him. "You don't know anything about Gina. I know her. Yeah, she made some big mistakes. At least she considers them mistakes. If she were to find out that I used similar methods as she did back then, I really would be blowing in the wind. So don't threaten me. It's really of no use."

"But you're scared of her." James shook his head. "What exactly is so scary about this female? It's not like she's that tough."

"That female has been around for more than six hundred years." Ricky stepped closer. "Think about all the things that she must have gone through and done in those years to survive. There aren't that many that know about our kind and how to kill us, but there are enough. Besides, she's just had to survive. I still say that I like my chances with her better."

"If it's what helps you sleep at night, or should I say, during the day." James smiled. He loved dealing with vampires. They were so easy to threaten. "Just make sure that all the loose ends are tied up. If word got out about what I did, The Company would be none too pleased. And they would come after me and whoever helped me in the process."

"That would be the least of your problems." Ricky began pacing again. "If Gina were to find out, and if Andrea were to find out, I wouldn't exist. And they wouldn't even be able to identify your body when Gina got through."

"Well, then." James turned his back on the vampire. "We best both keep our ends of the bargain. Looks like that's the only way we both survive." He quickly darted down the alleyway.

Ricky watched him go. His head was beginning to hurt. He hated having all these damn human emotions and foibles. It seemed that he had really done it this time. He was screwed no matter which way he went.

He turned to walk the other way. Another shadow caught his eye. "I know you're there. You might as well show yourself."

Gina made her way out of the shadows. "It sounds like you've been a very naughty boy. I'm just wondering what I'm going to do about that." She smiled as she made her way closer to him. With each step she took, his body shook more.

"What are we going to do?" Alicia held on tight to Andrea.

Andrea turned and did a half smile. "Aren't you some type of trained operative or something?" She squeezed her hand. "Do you have any type of weapons lying around?"

Alicia nodded and headed for the bedroom. Andrea followed closely behind her. "Not the circumstances I was hoping we'd be here under." She went to her closet. "What exactly are we talking about weapons wise?"

Andrea heard the door burst open. She peered out the bedroom door. Two fanged men entered. "I'd say wooden stakes, crosses, any of that you might have lying around."

"Vampires? What the hell are vampires doing attacking me?" Alicia shook her head. "Or are they coming after you? No, they wouldn't think to come here. What the hell is going on?"

"Less asking of questions, more getting of the weapons." Andrea made her way over to the closet. There were a lot of dresses and pantsuits hanging inside. "You really do have excellent taste." Her eyes spotted a rather revealing evening gown. Her mind went elsewhere for a moment. "Is there any other way out of here besides the front door?"

"Only the bathroom window and that's a little small. We'd have to squeeze through." There was a banging on the door. "And it doesn't sound like we have all that much time."

"There's only two that I could see. We could use the element of surprise." She came over and whispered in Alicia's ear. Alicia stood over by the queen-size bed.

Andrea mouthed, "Ready?" Alicia nodded.

Andrea opened the door. The first vampire went flying in. As he did, she tripped him and shoved him onto the bed. Alicia was waiting with her wooden stake. She used all her strength and found his heart through his back. The vampire was instantly turned to dust.

The second vampire quickly followed. He grabbed Andrea around the collar of her blue jean shirt. Slowly, he went for her neck. With her right hand, she pulled a crucifix from her back pocket. She held it to his face. He backed away and hissed at the same time.

She kept coming toward him. He kept backing up, looking for an opening. Andrea kept maneuvering him toward the couch in the living room. The vampire tripped over the end table, landing on his back. She got on top of him before he could recover. She placed the crucifix on his chest. There was an unpleasant sizzling sound.

"All right. You're gonna start talking. Or I'm going to leave that there all day and night." Andrea could feel that Alicia was standing right behind her. "Get something to tie Mr. Fangy up with. He's either gonna do some talking or he's going to be a pile of ashes like his friend."

"I'm not saying anything, bitch." He glared at her. "You think I'm scared of you. There are others that I'm more afraid of. Believe you me."

Andrea sighed as Alicia brought her some really thick ropes. "Have them laying around for business or pleasure?" Andrea's face reddened considerably. She never talked like this to another woman. What was her deal? And under the present circumstances, it was really unusual.

Alicia also reddened a little at the thought. "A good operative is always prepared for everything." She could not help but think, not everything. Falling in love was definitely not something The Company had prepared her for.

"Do you have some holy water?" Andrea finished tying up the vampire. She dragged him the short distance from the end table to the couch and laid him on it. "If he doesn't mind the singeing of the crucifix, maybe he won't be so thrilled with the whole burning sensation of the holy water."

"Yeah, I'll go get it." Alicia turned to go.

"Wait!" The vampire's eyes pleaded with her. "I'll talk. But you might as well dust me afterwards. If you don't, she will."

Alicia turned back around. "She who?"

"Gina."

"Why are you so scared, Ricky?" Gina was still coming at the vampire. "Are you afraid I overheard your conversation with Mr. James? You're right. I did."

"Please, don't kill me." Ricky began running.

"Stop now!" Gina launched herself at the fleeing vampire. In two strides, she overtook him. "I told you to stop."

"B-but you're going to…"

"Going to what?" Gina shook her head. "The only thing I want to know is if Andrea has found out about any of this. If you've at least not screwed that up, I can live with you dealing with James. I, as you know, have dealt with him in the past. Several times, in fact."

"She hasn't found out from me. Or anyone else that I know." Ricky shrugged. "I was just in it for the money. His and yours kinda meshed, if you know what I mean. I figure I might as well get some money out of the deal."

Gina shook her head. "You have really got to stop thinking and follow orders. It's going to be the death of you some day." She turned and began walking away from him.

Ricky quickly followed. "You mean, I'm still in?"

"For now. Have you gotten the warehouses setup yet?" Gina looked at him. "Or were you too busy running around with Mr. James all night long?"

"N-no, I got the warehouses ready before the meeting. That's why I was late." He tried to smile but simply looked ill instead.

"Well, it's nice to know I can sometimes count on you." She quickened her pace. "Something tells me I'd better find Andrea. We need to talk. I may just have to tell her what's going on. I hope she'll understand why I'm doing what I'm doing."

"Do you want me to take care of the operatives once they start showing up?"

"If you mean, by making them as comfortable as possible, yes." She glanced at him one more time. "Things are really getting messy. We all better be careful. It could easily be anyone of us that doesn't survive all of this."

Andrea's face was really pale. Alicia came over and put a hand on her back. "You can't be serious. Gina's behind this. Exactly what is it she has you doing?"

The vampire hesitated. Andrea grabbed the bottle of holy water from Alicia. "All right. All right." He swallowed hard. "Gina has us rounding up operatives. She doesn't want to hurt any of them, but she will. And since she's an operative," he pointed to Alicia, "we came here to get her. Gina told me to make sure and get her. She was in too deep and could really mess things up."

"I heard that much." Alicia looked at Andrea in surprise. "Well, not the part about you. That's where I was tonight. Gina, my special friend, and this group of vamps had a meeting setup. I wanted to find out what was going down. She was even talking about killing the operatives, about killing you. Only I didn't know it was you."

"Well, I knew I'd be a target." Alicia shrugged. "It's just the first time I knew about it first hand. It's kinda weird knowing that people are gunning for you."

Andrea turned back to the vampire. "There was something else she said. She wanted to set up a meeting with someone. Something about a feud between her and this man. Somebody, I assume, from The Company."

"Yeah." The vampire strained against the tight ropes. "Henry. She said that something happened and that it was time to settle the whole thing."

"Oh, God!" Now Alicia was turning a pale color. "Are you sure the name was Henry?" The vampire nodded. "Well, that's just wonderful."

Andrea turned her attention from the vampire to the redhead. "What's the matter? Is he somebody you know?"

"Yeah, I know him. He's my stepfather."

Henry was waiting inside a very luxurious hotel room. It was in the Marriott Suite. He was not so sure if it had been such a good idea to start following Alicia. And he was hearing rumors that James was not exactly on the up and up. It was time for a confrontation between the two.

James paused only for a moment when he saw Henry sitting at the dining room table. "Breaking and entering, I really didn't think it was your style, Henry."

"Well, we all do what we think is best for The Company, now don't we?" Henry stood, taking his glass of scotch with him. "And you seem to be doing more than others at the moment."

James raised his eyebrows as he made his way over to the mini bar. He poured himself a scotch and took a sip before turning to look at Henry. "And what exactly is that supposed to mean, my dear Henry?"

"Let's just say I've been doing some digging. It seems that I'm not the only one that has a personal interest in whether or not we can rid the earth of Gina."

"Whatever are you talking about?" James made his way and sat at the dining room table. "I know why you want her dead. The Company really doesn't care if she lives or dies unless she proves to be a nuisance. Like we have with many others that have become nuisances, we'll take care of her."

Henry came over and slammed his drink down on the table. "Are you threatening me, James?" His smile grew big. "Let's just say that if anything were to happen to me, there is some information that you wouldn't want The Company to get hold of. And they will, if I'm not around to see that it stays buried."

"Now who's threatening who?" James stood and glared. "We've been friends for a long time, Henry. And we've worked together even longer. I think we both know that we won't give up without a fight. Either of us. So why don't we try and work this out? Like two grown men should."

"I'm not aligning myself with you." Henry stood and started toward the door. "I just wanted to let you know that I know almost everything there is to know about you. And I know, if the others were to find out, they wouldn't be so happy." He slammed the door as he left.

James sighed. "I think I need to call in a special favor. I can't very well have anyone knowing my secrets running around now can I?"

❖

Andrea stood up quickly and made her way over to Alicia. She wrapped her up in a big hug. "I'm so sorry." She could feel that the other woman was beginning to cry. "We'll deal with this so that nobody gets hurt, I promise."

Alicia pulled out of the embrace. "That's not why I'm crying. I've put up with a lot of bullshit from the man the last three years. All about rules and regulations. Now it seems he's using The Company for some type of revenge on your friend Gina."

"I'm not so sure she's my friend." Andrea started toward the couch. She noticed the empty ropes lying on the floor. "Shit! Where is he?" She quickly turned to find Alicia in the clutches of the vampire. "You better let her go before I get anymore upset than I already am."

The vampire laughed. "And exactly what is an ordinary woman like yourself going to do to me?" He smiled. "Or have you forgotten that I have the super strength working for me."

"You may have super strength, but brains are rarely a vampire's best friend." Andrea smiled as she threw the bottle of holy water she had put in her back pocket at the loud mouthed vampire.

Alicia managed to duck enough not to get hit by the glass bottle. She did get wet as the glass shattered. The vampire instantly let go of Alicia as he began smoking readily. Andrea grabbed the wooden stake she had put in her shirt pocket. With as much force as she could muster, she plunged the stake into his heart. The vampire returned to the ashes that he once was.

"Sorry, I seem to have made a mess of your nice apartment." She walked over to where Alicia still stood. The redhead seemed a little stunned. "Are you all right, baby?"

The last word made her snap out of it. "So you've got a nickname for me already. Does this mean we're going steady?" She asked the question with a hopeful expression on her face.

"I wouldn't say I'm ready for total commitment here, but I think we do make a great team." She looked around the apartment and the mess that had become of it. "We're going to need a safe place to stay for a few days until we can figure things out."

"I think I know of somewhere we can go at least for the night."
Alicia came and stood face to face with the other woman. "It's about
half an hour drive, so we can talk and get to know each other better.
The real people."

"You mean, besides all those lies?" Andrea smiled as Alicia
nodded. She pulled the redhead closer. "So this is gonna be more than
just a little one time thing. Are we talking a relationship? Or am I just
dreaming?"

"Well, if it says anything, I'm bringing you home to meet my
mother."

The two were now headed west on I-96. Alicia was doing the
driving and wanted to surprise her new girlfriend with the location.
They had been doing a lot of talking on the way.

"So that's why Gina has been so important in your life." Andrea
nodded. "You've been on your own since you were eleven. That's
amazing."

"I went from one foster home to another. It was what you hear
about all the time." She shrugged. "I didn't have anyone I could count
on. Every time I went to another foster home, I went to a new school.
I never made any friends. But I always knew that Gina was out there
looking out for me."

Alicia nodded. "You've never had anybody to count on until now.
I promise you I won't hurt you again. Or at least try not to. And I'm
not holding back anything."

"If you still have your connections with The Company, there is
something I'd like you to look into for me." Alicia glanced over at the
sandy blonde. "You don't have to if you don't want to. It's just that…
"

"What?" Alicia turned her head back toward the road. "No matter
what it is, I'll try to help you find out the answer you're looking for.
If I still have connections. We know that Gina knows about me and
is after me. We just don't know what The Company does. What is it
you want me to look into for you?"

"Well, that night that Gina saved me, it sounded like my dad was into some shady dealings." Andrea sighed. "When I joined the force, I felt like I was really being watched. I couldn't understand it, besides the fact that maybe they were looking out for a fellow cop's kid."

"But you soon thought it was more than that?" Alicia was trying to take all of this in. There was already a lot happening.

"After a while, the memories became a little clearer." She did a small laugh. "It seems that my kid psyche blocked out the really painful memories. Before my mom died of cancer, she always told me what a good cop my father had been. But the things that were said in that alley that night made it sound like he was into some serious dirty dealings."

"You've never been able to uncover the truth?" Alicia took exit 77 into a little town called Portland. "And it's been almost twenty years. That's what I'd call a little suspicious."

"Exactly. It's like it's all being covered up." Andrea looked around her. "Wow! I haven't been here in years." She shrugged at the look. "One of the many foster homes."

"I grew up here." She turned right and headed north on Grand River Avenue. "Do you have any idea who would want to cover up something like this?"

Andrea shook her head. "That's the problem. One of the many I've faced the last twenty years. People aren't liking the questions I've been asking. I've even been hauled in and threatened with having my PI license taken away."

"Sounds like somebody with some authority. Or connections." Alicia turned onto Divine Highway and then onto Looking Glass Road. "It's only a couple more miles."

Andrea nodded absently. "Could this somebody be The Company? Or maybe someone else."

Alicia glanced at the other woman. "The Company does have that much power, at least the higher ups do. Are you thinking that it was them?"

"Them or Gina." Andrea shook her head. "I'm just not sure of anything right now. Except that you're in danger from someone who used to be my best friend, granted a vampire, but still had been good. I've been targeted in the past." She turned to her new girlfriend. "Do you think we have a past connection?"

Alicia pulled into a semi circle driveway that took you to the back of a two story L-shaped white farmhouse. There was a gray brick garage just to your left as you pulled in. She pulled up to a yellow jeep.

"Mom's here." Alicia sighed as she put the car in park. "With all that's going on, anything is possible at this point."

Andrea got out and looked around. There were three houses until a dirt road. On the other side, she could see two houses. There was a field in back of the house and across the road. It all looked so peaceful and serene. It was so far from the world that she lived in back in Lansing.

"You really sure your mom won't mind?" She glanced at her watch. There was just enough moonlight to see all of her surroundings. "It's almost four in the morning."

"If we're quiet, she'll never know." Alicia walked up to the back door and used her key to unlock it. "Mom always told me I could stay any time I needed to." She motioned for the other woman to follow her in.

They entered a little walk in area with a table. It quickly lead to a spacious kitchen. Alicia took her hand and took the lead. They went from the kitchen to a dining room area. There were two doors side by side. Alicia took the one on the left.

They walked up a winding stairway. At the top, there were four different doors. "Mom's room," she whispered as she pointed to the first door on the left. "My room." She pointed to the third door from the left.

Both made their way in. Andrea stood staring around the room. It was long and narrow. There was a closet at the far end. The small twin bed was right at the end of the closet. A television sat under the far window.

"This was your room?" Andrea whispered.

"Yeah, not much I know." Alicia went and sat on the bed. There was no other furniture except for a dresser. She patted the bed next to her. "Join me."

Andrea smiled. But she did not move. "The beds kinda small for the two of us. I'll just use the floor."

Alicia stood up and took both Andrea's hands in her own. "Don't be silly. The bed is plenty big enough. Besides, we're just going to sleep, right?"

"I…" Andrea's face reddened. "I didn't mean it like that."

"I know. It's just fun to see you get flustered." She pulled the other woman over to the bed. "Sorry but my fantasy of the two of us together for the first time doesn't include my mother right next door."

Both women got into bed, Andrea first, with Alicia laying her head on her chest. "You've had fantasies already?"

"Oh, yeah." She took her hand and traced a little pattern on the other woman's stomach. "Trust me when I say you'll find out once we figure out what's going on. And my mother isn't next door."

"Can't wait for that day."

Gina slammed Ricky into the wall for the fifth time. There were a dozen humans looking on in terror. "What do you mean she's nowhere to be found? She has to be somewhere in this city."

Ricky landed hard on the ground when she let him go. Blood was flowing from his lip and his nose. "I'm telling you what I know. She's not anywhere that I've looked."

"Did she just simply disappear?" She shook her head. "Damn! She probably found out and is lying low somewhere. This is the last thing I wanted." She began pacing. "All I wanted to do was to get that damn Henry off my back and make sure that James stayed in line."

"Things are getting a little out of hand." Ricky was busy wiping the blood from his nose.

"You think?" Gina shook her head. "All of this is getting out of control. Now I may not have Andrea anymore." She picked up a heavy metal chair and threw it at the wall. There were screams from the on lookers. "Are these all the operatives on the list that I gave you?" She pointed to the group huddling together.

"Sure thing, boss." Finally having gotten the bleeding to stop, he ventured a little closer to the other vampire. "Except for the one you really wanted."

A huge growl escaped from Gina's throat. "You mean the one that was getting close to Andrea?" Ricky nodded as he backed away. "And where are the others?"

"Others?" Ricky nodded. "Right, well, Sly and Rick haven't come back. They were the ones that were supposed to get Alicia."

"Has anyone checked her apartment? Has anyone tried to locate that one?" Ricky shook his head. "Damn, this is why I always work alone. Nobody else can think for themselves." She turned to the vampire. "Get two of the others to go with you. Find out where she is. Maybe she knows where Andrea is."

Ricky looked at the sky through the one window in the warehouse. It was already starting to show the first signs of daylight. "But it's almost morning."

"Well, I guess you'd better hurry." Gina smiled at him. "Unless you'd like to stay and deal with me. That could be arranged. It would be nice to have something to take my frustrations out on."

"I'm outta here." Ricky took off like a shot.

"Creep." Gina turned toward the humans watching her. "You won't be hurt if your boss comes through. But we know how Mr. Henry works, so don't hold your breath."

She turned quickly and made her way to the entranceway. Before she left, she turned to the female vampire on guard. "Stay. Guard them. Don't hurt them. I'll be back when I'm back."

The scent of something delicious made Andrea wake up. She looked around the room quickly to remind herself where she was. Alicia was nowhere to be seen.

She stretched and slowly made her way down the stairs. The smell became stronger as she opened the door to the down stairs. There was a light coming from the kitchen. That was where she headed.

Standing in front of the stove was a little blacked haired woman with hints of gray in her hair. She smiled at her before she even stepped into the kitchen. Alicia was standing to the left in front of the sink holding a cup of coffee.

"Want some?" Alicia asked.

"Please." She walked over to the stove. "You must be Alicia's mother. I'm Andrea."

"I know." She smiled at the look she received. "I've heard quite a lot about you. It's nice to finally meet you."

Alicia shook her head as she handed Andrea a cup of coffee. "Forgive her. Subtly has never been one of her strong suits."

"What?" the dark haired woman asked. "I'm not to be a happy mother meeting the woman that…"

"That's enough, Mom." Alicia began to turn a little red.

"No, please do go on. I'd like to hear what your mom thinks." Andrea laughed at the look Alicia shot her.

The dark-haired woman held out her hand. "You can call me Eleanor." She looked and winked at her daughter. "Maybe before too long you can start calling me Mom as well."

"Mother, really, you are too much." Alicia made her way out to the kitchen table.

"It's nice to meet you, Eleanor." Andrea started out to the table as well. "I'm hoping I'll be able to call you Mom, someday." Andrea finished walking to the table and sat down.

Alicia shook her head. "You really enjoyed that, didn't you?" She could not help but laugh.

"Sorry, but teasing you feels really good."

Eleanor brought out two big plates full of scrambled eggs, toast, and sausage.

"Thanks! This smells and looks good."

"I try my best." Eleanor looked from Andrea to Alicia. "I'll be in the living room should you need anything else. You two try and come up with something so that you're both safe."

Andrea raised her eyebrows. "Was I really asleep that much longer than you? Did you tell her everything?"

Alicia shook her head. "No. She just knows that there's trouble and it has to do with The Company."

"She knows about The Company?" Andrea sounded really surprised. She picked up her coffee cup and took a sip.

"Well, Henry was working there when they met." The redhead shrugged. "Also, she tried to talk me out of joining when Henry recruited me. I should have listened to my mother."

Andrea laughed. "God! This feels so unreal. I'm so comfortable and happy here. It feels strange that there are people out to get the both of us."

"We can't stay here for long." Alicia took a sip of her coffee. "Mom realizes it, too. We're putting her in danger. I don't want that."

Andrea reached across the small table and took her hand. "Neither do I. We'll figure something out. But one thing I do know is that I'm not running. If we start running, we'll never be able to stop. Besides, I want to take out all the baddies."

"Baddies?" Alicia asked with a smile.

"What can I say? I watch too much television." Andrea took a bite of her eggs. "I'm wondering if I shouldn't call Gina."

Alicia practically slammed her coffee cup down. "What? Are you insane?"

"Just hear me out." Andrea leaned in closer. "If we can really figure out what Gina's up to, then maybe we can figure out what The Company is up to. Do you feel like having a conversation with your stepfather?"

"Not particularly." She sighed. "But I think you're right. If we can call from a payphone or something, we won't have a fixed location. They'll only know where we've been. And we do need to find out what's going on or at least what they want to tell us."

"Exactly." The sandy blond shook her head. "If Gina is doing what it appears she is, it won't be a picnic for me, either. But we've both got to do this. I want you safe. I want us to be able to start a life together." She reddened at the last statement.

"It's what I want, too." The redhead smiled. "The sooner the better."

James looked at the ten men assembled around him. It was an impressive group. The head of each of the offices of The Company was sitting around a large oval redwood table in the conference room on the top floor of the Lansing headquarters on Capital Street. He, of course, was sitting at the head.

"Gentleman, it is so nice that you have joined me." He looked around at the group of ten men. "It is imperative that we all are on the same wavelength."

A portly man in a charcoal-gray business suit sat up and leaned against the large table. "It seems that you have let things get out of hand, James. And why isn't Henry included in this meeting? I assume he's still very much a part of The Company. At least, last I checked."

"Irving, he is but," James stood and began pacing. "I hate to be the one to say this, but I believe his personal interests are getting in the way of his better judgement."

"Are we talking about his daughter or the vampire?" The man who spoke was dressed very casually compared to the others. He was also half the age of most of the men gathered. "It might make a difference in deciding on how to deal with him."

"Sedrick. That's the problem." James turned to the youngest member of the group. "It's both. He still wants to get rid of the vampire in any way possible. And Alicia seems to be turning on us and getting involved with her assignment again."

A man named David shook his head. "Why are we just hearing about all this now? Shouldn't we have been kept in the loop? I mean this affects all of our operations. Not just the Lansing branch. If we have a rogue operative, it could prove problematic at best."

"And speaking for the main headquarters," a bald man with a goatee ventured, "we should be kept apprized of everything. Or have you forgotten the mission? We are to rid the planet of every vampire and demon we come across. Why have you let this Gina run ramped in your city, James?"

"We, at first, thought she could help keep the vampire population down. Her goal seemed to be the same as ours." James shook his head. "We were fools, but it seemed that she was actually helping the cause. But now, it seems she has joined the ranks of the others."

David slammed down his hand hard on the desk. "You've really screwed this whole thing up, James." He turned to the others in the group. "Perhaps one of us should stay on and take over this operation until we can find somebody more suitable."

James quickly returned to the head of the table. "I assure you, gentlemen, I have a plan that will take care of all of this. You can count on me." A knock on the door interrupted his speech. "Excuse me." He walked over to the door and received a note and some papers. He read it as he returned to the table. "I'm afraid things have gotten even worse."

"Why does that not surprise me?" the man in the goatee asked.

"What is it, James? What is happening?" Sedrick looked very nervous.

"It appears Gina has decided to take the fight to us." James sighed as he handed them each a copy of a letter from Gina. "Basically it states that we are to call off our vendetta against her or she will take matters into her own hands. She now has a dozen of our operatives in her clutches."

Finally, the most senior man of the group spoke. "You really have done it this time, James. We have no choice but to do as she asks. We can't lose any operatives. It's too hard to recruit these days."

"I disagree." James stood straighter. "If you'll listen to me, I think we can agree that my plan will succeed. And with minimal casualties." At the looks he received, he continued. "After all, we are fighting a war, gentlemen. And casualties are a part of war."

Henry paced in his luxurious apartment. As Alicia would say, a family of twelve could live in it. But he was all alone and feeling more and more alone. From his contacts, he had heard of a meeting of the highest officials in The Company. He had always been informed of, if not invited to, these meetings.

He seemed to be on his own now. He only had a few contacts left. And they would not be willing to risk their own careers just to help him out. He knew how they all felt about him. It was a silly vendetta against Gina. But she had killed his only son. Granted, he had been turned into a damn vampire.

Henry made his way to the patio. He opened the door and took in the bright morning sun. The springtime air smelled so clean and pure. But he knew what lay beneath all that. The sewers were now teaming with an untold number of the undead. After all, the sun was shining very bright.

He took a few more deep breaths to try and clear his head. His stepdaughter seemed to be betraying him and The Company. And he was not any closer to finding where Gina was. No matter the tactics he used, she would not show herself. Not even his most recent attempt, going after the one person she cared most about had had the desired affect.

There was a knock on the door, startling him from his thoughts. He quickly closed and locked the patio door. As he made his way to the door, he glanced around the spacious apartment. There were so many fine things. But it meant nothing if he had no one to share it with.

Before opening the door, he peered out the peephole. It was his friend Elliot from The Company. Elliot was a young man, still just starting to make his way up the treacherous ranks of The Company.

Henry quickly opened the door. "Elliot, this is indeed quite the surprise." He moved aside so that the young man could enter.

"I shouldn't be telling you this, but…" Elliot handed him an envelope. "And the tail that was requested on Alicia, they lost her as she got onto I-96."

The older man nodded. "Thank you. Now get out of here."

"But I…" Elliot looked hurt and confused.

"I may be on the outs with The Company." Henry put his hand on the younger man's shoulder. "Should they discover this meeting, you could be finding yourself in some serious trouble. Again, I thank you for being a good friend. I just don't want you in the same trouble that I am in."

Elliot nodded his head. "I . . . " He smiled. "You taught me what this job is about. If something should happen, I'll never regret my decision to join after you recruited me. I'll always be grateful to you for everything." He started toward the door.

"You are my prized pupil." Henry made his way to the door. "Be careful. Things are getting very serious." The young man nodded and walked out the door.

Henry locked and bolted the door. He made his way to the dining room table and sat down. There was a feeling like somebody was watching him. He shrugged it off as he opened the envelope. It was a report stating that a dozen operatives had gone missing and that Alicia was also nowhere to be found. It did not really say what or who was behind the disappearances of that many operatives. But Henry knew.

Anything to do with the damn vampire and he knew. It was like they had become connected after what she had done. Sometimes, he even felt he could feel her pain and know her thoughts. It was not exactly like that this time. He just knew that she was behind whatever was going on. And he knew how James and the others would handle it. And that would lead to a lot of the operatives' deaths.

The phone rang, again startling him from his thoughts. He quickly made his way to the stand by the sofa where the phone was. "Hello?"

"It's your daughter. Is it safe to talk?" Alicia's strong voice was on the other end.

"Alicia, where the hell are you, and what's going on?" Henry's voice boomed through the telephone wires.

"I'm assuming you know then about the others and me."

Henry sighed. "Not exactly. All I know is that twelve operatives are missing. And you are pretty much being labeled a traitor at this point. What is going through that redhead of yours? Didn't you learn anything from the last time?"

Now Alicia sighed. "Calm down. In a way, I'm glad that I'm on the outs. Maybe I can actually get something done now. All I need to know from you, do they suspect me of anything? And what are they going to do about Gina?"

"They'll do what they do, no matter the cost. Especially now that James is in charge." He let himself fall onto the sofa. "As far as you, they're looking for you. They want to know what you know and why you haven't checked in. I'd say you have about eight more hours before you are truly labeled a traitor. And you know the power of The Company and what that would mean."

"Yes, I do. After all, you taught me well." She hesitated before continuing. "I think you should know. I am not going to work for The Company anymore. I'll try not to involve you anymore. I do have a favor to ask."

"I'm afraid I'm all out of favors." Henry began raising his voice. "Because of you, I'm now considered an outsider. I'm having to find things out from Elliot. Are you happy?"

"I'm real happy." Alicia's voice got strained. "I'm on the run, possibly for my life. You're telling me your situation isn't much better. Oh, yeah, Dad, I'm real happy."

"Damn it!" Henry stood and began pacing. "Why couldn't you just follow orders like a good operative? Why couldn't you just leave well enough alone?"

"A good operative always asks questions." Alicia took a deep breath. She did not want to get into a shouting match with him. "Sorry I've never followed the rules. But there are gray areas out there. It's not as simple as good and bad. Even you should realize that by now."

"There are no gray areas. Only what you want to make of them." He stopped his pacing. "And you are with that woman, aren't you?"

"God, Dad." Alicia could feel the anger swelling up. "Me being gay has nothing to do with this. I would have eventually come to the same conclusions about The Company. She just opened my eyes a little faster, that's all. Besides, I thought you'd be happy for me. After all, you know what it's like to be alone."

"I wasn't alone before you went and did your stupid disappearing act. Please, just come back. We can work things out. I promise."

"Yours and The Company's promises don't interest me. I've got somebody I can trust. Can you say the same thing?"

Henry slammed the phone down. The thought that he had himself and that it was enough entered his mind. He just wondered if it would be enough.

Alicia stared at the phone before hanging it up. She turned to see Andrea looking at her with a worried look. Alicia smiled before she said, "I wasn't really expecting any different."

Andrea came up and brought her into a big hug. They were just outside the Arby's restaurant in Portland just before you got back onto I-96. "Still, it's not that easy. You may know the words that are coming, but it's still hard to listen to them."

They stood for the longest time just holding each other. Alicia slowly pulled out of the embrace. "I don't know if you got it from my end of the conversation, but I'm basically out. I have no one that I can trust." She quickly added. "With The Company, of course." She smiled at her girlfriend. "And if we don't act fast, The Company is going to do its usual and that means sending in a special OPS team."

"That sounds not good." Andrea shook her head. "That could very easily lead to some casualties. This is sounding not good. Not good at all."

"Maybe you could talk to Gina and warn her." Andrea looked surprised. "I'm not saying that what she has done is right, but we could save some innocent lives. You could tell her that Henry is on the outs as well. This won't get her the meeting she wants. If anything, it will only make them go after her. More than ever."

"I was gonna call and find out what was really going on anyway. Guess now I have to do the warning thing." She turned to the payphone. "My turn."

"I'll get us something to eat. It's after noon already. I'll be inside if you need anything."

Andrea watched her for a long time before she dialed. She used her phone card so that it would be harder to trace. It did not take long for Gina to answer. "It's Andrea. We need to talk."

"Do you want to talk over the phone or face to face?" There was a strain in her voice that Andrea had never heard before.

"I'm really not up for a meeting. Not yet."

"So you do know what I've been up to." Gina growled deep in her throat.

"I know some things you have been up to." She hesitated. This was not going to be that informational. She had to make sure that those people were safe. "You've got to let the operatives go. They and you are in serious danger."

"And from whom?" Gina was not liking the sound of the conversation. "You're with that woman, and she is filling your head with ideas."

"I am with Alicia. In every way. But…" Andrea sighed. "That's not why I'm calling. She found out from her one last contact with The Company that they are going to use a special OPS force to get the operatives back that you kidnaped."

"And this is supposed to scare me in someway." Gina laughed. "You used to know me better than that."

"I thought I knew you. But you've either changed or I never really knew you in the first place." Andrea swallowed hard. "I think I still have that image of the mysterious woman who came to my rescue so many years ago. A little late to save my daddy, but you still rescued me. And now, I hear you are kidnaping people just to get your point across. And now you won't believe me when I say you are in danger and putting the lives of those you have in danger. What the hell has happened to you?"

"Me?" Gina laughed. "You seem to be the one to forget all the things I've done for you. I am not going to harm these people. I give you my word on that."

"The only way these people are going to be safe is if you let them go." Andrea hit her fist against the wall, garnering many looks from inside, including Alicia. She stared at her throbbing hand a moment before continuing. "These special OPS that are coming, they will use any force necessary to take you and anyone you have working for you out. They will not be so concerned with the safety of their compatriots. Will you be?"

"How can you ask me that?" Gina again growled low in her throat. "If you say that the lives of these somewhat innocent people are in danger, I will let them go. And what about you? Do you still believe that I am good?"

"I wish I could say yes." Andrea leaned against the wall. Alicia started to get up. Andrea held up a hand. "Listen, the other thing I wanted to tell you, if you'll believe me, is that Henry is no longer a prominent member of The Company. But because of your actions, you are a bigger target than before. So be careful."

"You still believe enough in me to warn me about all of this. Do you think we will ever be able to regain the trust we once had?"

"I wish I knew."

Gina slammed her phone shut the minute she heard the all too familiar sound of a vampire turning into dust. She ran toward the entrance. But it was too late. All the remaining vampires were now dust. That left her to fight all alone. She quickly turned toward the group of captives she had. In one quick move, she unlocked the cage and swung the door open.

"Your friends are here. Tell them I'm gone." Gina made her way to the window of the warehouse. The sun was pouring down on her. She picked up the blanket she had set there, just in case. Using one of the boxes that were piled around, she launched herself out the window.

She could hear shouts and screams coming from behind her as she smashed through the glass. The blanket slipped off her for a moment causing her skin to begin smoking. She quickly wrapped herself up again.

Before she took off for the sewer entrance, she heard the explosion. It sent her flying to the ground. When she looked back at the warehouse, it was in flames. And she could hear more screams coming from inside.

She made her way to the sewer drain and lowered herself in. Her vampire eyes quickly adjusted to the darkness. The sound of footsteps sent her into running. It would not take them long to discover which drain she had used for escape.

Her long strides made great progress. It was not long until she was under Andrea's office. She used the secret opening to pull herself out of the sewer. She looked around. It was clear that Andrea had not been there in at least a day. Her scent was almost gone from the room.

The door opened and Adam walked in. He stopped in his tracks as he saw Gina. He let out his breath. "You scared me." He took in the expression on her face. "Has something happened to Andrea? I haven't heard from her since yesterday morning. Not unusual, but still."

"She hasn't told you what's going on?" Adam shook his head. "That's good. That's very good. If people should ask questions about her, tell them as little as possible. They'll probably try to get persuasive. If they do, just tell them what you know. Especially if they ask about me."

"What exactly is going on?" Adam looked totally confused.

"Just believe me when I say the less you know the better." Gina made her way to the secret entrance. "Be careful, Adam. Things are getting dangerous. For everyone." She slid slowly down into the darkness below.

He stared after her for a few minutes before he returned to the outer office. Two men in business suits with guns were waiting for him.

"We'll have to get going soon." Alicia watched as Andrea picked at her food. "It's all right if you still want to trust her. Maybe you still can."

Andrea looked up. "It's just so much more complicated than I thought. She sounded like she was going to let the people go. But I get the feeling that she still wants to go after your father and The Company. I'm just wondering at what cost?"

"Listen, I know somewhat how you're feeling." Andrea looked her in the eyes. "It's not the same, but I really did admire my stepfather. But he's betraying me and he can't even see it. He's putting revenge before anything else. Maybe that's what is happening with Gina."

Andrea shrugged. "All I know is that she's not the same person that I met almost twenty years ago. Something happened, besides her saving me. Something before she saved me. And I think it's coming back to haunt her."

"Did you say twenty years ago?" Alicia's eyes widened in thought as Andrea nodded. "My stepbrother was killed twenty years ago. I was only seven at the time. The weird thing about it was they had him cremated."

"What's so weird about that?" Andrea looked a little confused.

"Well, Henry is really into traditions. There's a family cemetery in Portland. All of his family is buried there." The redhead thought for a moment. "Henry supposedly spread Fredrick's ashes in the cemetery but still. It's not the same as the family tradition of being buried with the others."

"You're not trying to put a connection with Gina and Henry, are you?" Andrea sat back and tried to put her thoughts together. "Although, it would make some sense. Gina seemed upset that she couldn't save my father. She told me that saving people is what she did. Maybe she couldn't save your stepbrother."

"You feel like doing some digging?" Alicia asked, already knowing the answer.

"What exactly do you have in mind?" Andrea smiled a small smile. The detective thing was definitely her thing.

"Well, if we can maybe find a connection between Henry and Gina, that would explain his possible vendetta." Alicia shrugged.

"And that would be why Gina has never let go, either." Andrea quickly stood up. "If Gina thought that Henry would never give up on

78

his vendetta, she would try almost anything to get him to stop. Maybe that's what the kidnaping was all about."

"Only one way to find out. We need information and access to a computer." Alicia stood up as well. Both headed for the door. "I'm thinking library."

The group of men still sat around the large oval table. James was standing looking at the traffic below. The group of eleven, including himself, was waiting for confirmation.

That was when there was a knock on the door. "Gentlemen, this should be what we've been waiting for." James quickly made his way to the door. The same woman handed him an envelope and quickly walked away. "Here is what happened." He opened the envelope and gave each man a copy.

"Dear, Lord!" Sedrick was the first to react to the report. "I know we agreed on special OPS, but this is not what I had in mind. This is unacceptable."

"I concur." Kirk, the most senior of those in the room added. "I've been a part of this organization longer than any of you. Let me tell you something, gentlemen. A loss of this many good people is unacceptable. And it's going to be hard to explain that many dead people from an organization that is supposed to be about charity."

"You'll get no arguments from anybody in this room." David turned to face James. "Except for probably our illustrious leader of the Lansing branch."

"Come now, gentlemen. You are forgetting what's at stake." James made his way to the head of the table and sat down. "We are what stands between evil taking over the earth and untold chaos. And people have a blind eye to the things that go on. I assure you that the operatives did what was necessary."

"Perhaps." Irving looked around at the group. "But according to this, your operatives are almost certain that Gina escaped. Was it really worth the lives of twelve of your people, even if we had managed to capture or kill the one vampire?"

James shook his head. "You, gentlemen, have not been out on the front lines in a long time. You each sit in your offices and give nice and easy orders. Do you even read how many people each day are hurt or killed by vampires? The numbers are staggering. And you sit there in judgement of my methods. According to this report, sixteen vampires were killed. Sixteen to twelve. Not the greatest percentage, but I still believe it was for the best."

Finally, Kirk stood and faced the men gathered. "He's right." All faces turned and stared at him. "I've been reading our casualty rates. The epidemic of vampires is growing by leaps and bounds. We may have to adjust our way of dealing with the undead. I believe we have found just the man to do so. I suggest we go back to our perspective offices and watch and learn from James. If his methods prove as effective as I believe they will, we'll implement them in all of our offices. Any objections?"

James was met with only silence. "Thank you for your confidence in me. I'm honored." He nodded to each of the men.

"Just don't abuse the power we have given you." Kirk stood and made his way to the door. "It can easily be taken away if your methods should prove unworthy."

Adam felt himself being dragged along a cold tile floor. His head was pounding, and there was a blindfold over his eyes. He tried saying something only to realize that they had also put a gag in his mouth. The last thing he remembered was those two guys in business suits with guns. This must be what Andrea had tried warning him about when she hired him.

He had laughed at her. The thought that anyone would try and get information out of him or use him to get to her was just absurd. After all, he was just her secretary. He did not even know about half of her operations. She wanted it that way to keep him safe or at least try to keep him safe.

Well, so much for safe. He felt two hands grab his arms roughly. Soon, his body was launched in the air. His body landed with a thud in the corner of the room. His head hit one of the walls, making it pound even more. A door slammed shut.

It was not long before he heard footsteps. He could hear the door open and shut. The footsteps quickly made their way over to where he was laying. He could sense someone standing in front of him, someone that had a lot of anger. The anger was radiating off from whoever it was.

"Adam?" He looked up where the male voice was coming from. "We don't want to hurt you, boy. We just want to know how to contact your boss. If you do that, we will gladly let you go."

Adam scrunched further into the corner. He was so not liking the vibe he was getting from the guy. One thing he had learned from Andrea, trust no one. He really had not liked that philosophy but at the moment, it made the most sense. After all, there was still the possibility of a gun or guns.

"I'm so sorry." The gag was roughly removed from his mouth. "You can't possibly answer if you are still gagged. Now, tell me how to contact Miss Freemont or Miss Walker. If you don't, we will have to take different tactics."

"I-I'm not telling you anything." His voice came up out roughly. His throat hurt with every syllable it was so dry.

"Now don't try the hero act." Adam suddenly felt a hand around his throat. "You are expendable. Don't think that Andrea doesn't know that. Do you think she really cares if you live or die?" There was a cruel laugh that echoed throughout the room. "You had better give us the information we seek. The consequences could be deadly. Very deadly."

Adam swallowed hard. Andrea had always told him to just tell whatever it is that people wanted to know. She did not want him putting himself in a grave situation. Knowing he had no real choice, he cleared his throat. "I'm not sure where she is."

The hand tightened a little for a few minutes. Slowly, it loosened. "We figured as much. But you always know how to contact her. Tell us before we lose our patience."

Adam shook his head and sighed. He did not want to give in. But if he did not, it would mean they would probably definitely kill him. He inhaled sharply as he felt something cold and sharp at his throat.

"We're not going to ask again." The voice was full of annoyance.

"Fine." Adam again sighed. "The only way I know how to get in touch with her is through her cell phone."

"That would be just perfect."

"Wow!" Andrea was staring around the main lobby of the Michigan State Library. The gray marble was very impressive. As was the thirty-foot blue spruce surrounded by glass that was in the middle of the entrance.

"This way." Alicia took her hand and lead her to the elevators. "You've never been here?"

Andrea shrugged. "I stick to lower rent places, I guess. Besides, I have a contact or two at The Lansing State Journal. You'd be surprised what journalists will do for a story."

Alicia smiled in response. "Well, welcome to the twenty-first century." The elevator arrived. "Second floor."

When the elevators opened again, they were in a huge library full of people. The center had a cluster of computers for internet research. Over in the corner, there was a room that said "Newspaper Archives."

Andrea headed toward the archives room. Alicia took her hand and made her stop. She pointed to the computers. "Faster and more information, remember?"

"Maybe for a brainiac like you." Andrea shook her head. "You let your fingers do the talking. I'm going to do things the old-fashioned way."

"Sure it's safe to separate?" Alicia looked a little worried at the thought.

"I'll be next door." Andrea pulled her into a hug. "I'm not letting anything happen to you. That's the whole point of this. The more information we can get our hands on, the better."

"Then we can get our hands on each other." Alicia quickly kissed her girlfriend. She smiled as she saw her cheeks reddening quite a bit. "You're sexy when you blush."

Andrea watched her for a moment before heading back to the newspapers. She shook her head to clear it. This woman was definitely different from any other she had gone out with before. And it was only day three that they had known each other. It was just so unreal.

She sat herself at the computer and smiled to herself. Even doing the newspaper thing would require using a computer. That was the world that she lived in now. She typed in the keywords and waited for the search to be completed.

The detective in her looked around her. There was only one other person in the room. The person was wearing a name tag that said Ester. The lady was older and very tall. She made a mental note. It was sad how she was suspicious of everybody. But that was the way in her line of work.

The computer beeped, indicating it had finished its search. She printed out the results. There were three articles that caught her interest.

Andrea made her way to the back of the room. That was where the articles from twenty years ago were kept. She found the article dated May twelfth, the day after her birthday. She had tried before to look up this article. But everywhere she went, the pages had been torn out but not here. She was finally going to be able to see what somebody did not want her to see.

Last night, thirty five-year-old officer Alexander F. Freemont was killed while on an outing with his eleven-year-old daughter. While police are labeling it a gang attack, sources are saying that it might have been some type of retaliation. It was suspected by many on the force that Mr. Freemont was into some things that were illegal. While these reports cannot be confirmed or denied, the evidence was mounting. A source inside the police's Internal Affairs was pointing that an arrest may soon have been made. If reports are accurate, Mr. Freemont was heavily into the local drug trade.

Sources state that his main dealings included marijuana, cocaine, and heroine. His daughter is now an orphan and will be put into foster care. This story will be watched closely and updated when there are more details.

Andrea stared at the article. She read it again. Her instincts had been right. Her father had been into some dirty dealings with those evil vampires. Was Gina also involved? She shook her head trying to clear it.

She searched, but that was it. For the next three months, there were no follow up stories. It was as if somebody had buried the story. It made sense. Somebody was trying to keep the truth from her or maybe even the world.

Even though her heart was aching at the thought of her father and dirty dealings, she knew she had to keep going. There were two more articles she felt she needed to look at. Before she got the articles, she noticed that Ester was still hovering around. It was starting to give her a bad feeling in the pit of her stomach. And that was usually a bad sign.

Quickly, she got the next two on her list. Something was telling her that it was not safe for her. Her mind wandered out to Alicia. At least she was where there were people. Usually, the baddies did not try anything in a crowd.

She scanned the next article. Her eyes widened and she nearly threw up, she became so sick. And she felt that she knew who was behind the article.

Authorities are at a loss to explain the theft of blood from the local blood banks. This is the first time in history that any such theft has occurred. Sources say that police have no leads and are not even sure where to start. Alexander F. Freement had been investigating these thefts at the time of his death.

This was huge. Somebody was into stealing blood. And there were more thefts after that. Every few weeks, there were more thefts reported. Suddenly, after May eleventh, the same night Gina rescued her, the thefts stopped. Was it because she had stopped the thieves or was it because she was trying to cover her own tracks? There was one more article to look up. It was about Alicia's stepfather.

Henry Dupie, a well-respected business man, has requested that a special on campus security force be implemented immediately. His son was tragically killed when warring gangs were fighting over drug territory. He especially warned that there was a female leader of one of the gangs. She was the one that killed his son, according to some of the witnesses....

Well, that certainly did clench it. Gina was the one that had killed Alicia's stepbrother. But did she do it just because? Andrea shook her head. She was still having a hard time believing that Gina would do things like that. She had to have a reason. And about stealing the blood, there had to be an explanation. Things were not as simple as they seemed.

Andrea gathered her notes that she had made. She looked around again. The woman was nowhere to be seen. Her heart skipped a beat, and she quickly made her way out of the archive room and to where Alicia should still be at the computers.

Instead of finding Alicia, she found her purse and some notes. There was no way that she would have left that. Her mind was trying to panic. She was already so in love with the woman that she was having trouble keeping her focus.

There was a scream that came from the direction of the elevators. It instantly made her mind focus. She ran over just in time to see Alicia with the strange woman. And there was something dark pressing against her side. The elevator doors closed before she could move. Like a bolt of lightning, she was making her way down the stairs.

Before the elevator made it to the main floor, Andrea was standing just to the side. She heard the bing and flattened herself against the smooth gray marble wall. Alicia was the first off the elevator, like Andrea knew she would be.

Before the woman could take a step off the elevator, Andrea grabbed her arm. Shattering gray marble on the other side of the hallway told Andrea that the gun had gone off but with no sound. The woman must have a silencer. She took the woman's arm and banged it against her knee. The gun fell to the floor with a dull thud.

The woman pushed Alicia, sending her flying onto Andrea. Both women ended up on the ground lying face to face. Alicia's eyes were more than a little scared. Andrea took her into a hug. She watched over Alicia's shoulder as Ester made her way toward the exit. She could feel her girlfriend's heart racing. She kissed her on the neck. "Damn!" Andrea realized her heart was racing, too. It was so strange, but now she was so totally connected to this woman. If she hurt, then Andrea hurt. "Are you all right, baby?"

Alicia took a deep breath. She held tight to Andrea's strong body. "You saved me." Her voice was a little weak. At least her breathing was returning to normal.

"I wouldn't have had to if I would have followed my darn instincts." Alicia finally pulled away, wearing a quizzical look on her face. "I just got this vibe from that woman. She was watching me while I was in the archive room." They were inches apart. She let her lips brush against the redhead's. "When you weren't there, I got so scared. I just knew something had happened. And if it did, it would have been my fault."

"Nonsense. I'm the one that supposedly has operative training. I guess The Company doesn't train us as well as I'd like to brag." She smiled. There were suddenly a lot of people standing in the hallway. "We better get my stuff and talk about what we found out."

Andrea noticed the people as well. She stood up and helped Alicia up as well. As discreetly as she could, she picked up the gun and hid it under her jacket. Both got on to the elevator and went back to the computers. Luckily, all the things that Alicia had been researching were still there.

"We better not talk here." Andrea looked around. There were too many strange faces. Who knew which one would try something next. "Just not sure where to go."

Alicia sighed. "Do you have some cash on you?" Andrea raised her eyebrows. "If we have enough money, we could get a hotel room for a couple nights. But we'd have to use cash so that we weren't traceable."

Andrea nodded. "That's a good idea." She looked in her wallet. "Not much, but it will at least give us a night. How about you?"

A smile crept across Alicia's face. "We operatives are always prepared." She pulled out at least four hundred dollars.

"You just wanted to see how much was in my wallet." Andrea shook her head. "I can at least spring for dinner."

"We still have that date coming." Andrea looked at her questioningly. "Remember. You. Me. Trippers." Now Andrea smiled. "Won't be able to talk much there, but...."

"It will be fun. And with all that's going on, we need a little distraction. And a public place is a good hideout." Andrea took her girlfriend's hand. "Let's get out of here before the next operative shows up." Before leaving, Andrea looked around again. It was as if there was a familiar presence, one that used to give her a lot of comfort. She shook her head, trying to clear it. Slowly, she walked hand in hand with Alicia toward the elevators.

Out of the archives room, a familiar tall dark-haired woman appeared. Her face was a look of sadness and pain. She could not believe what had just happened. She had witnessed all that Andrea had discovered and the ensuing little battle. Her Andrea seemed lost to her. She did not need Gina's protection anymore. In fact, she was now the one doing the protecting.

There was a low growl in her throat. There was still one thing that she could do for Andrea. She could protect her at any cost from The Company. And show her that the woman she was falling in love with could not be trusted. If it was the last thing she did, she would show Andrea the real person hiding behind the lies.

James made his way out of the room that Adam was tied up in. He smiled at the thought of the little cowardly boy lying there for eternity. There was no way that he was ever going to see the light of day again, only possibly as bait.

He slowly made his way back to his office on the fifth floor. The others had left an hour before. That left him in charge to run things the way he saw fit. The Company was headed in a whole new and improved direction.

The only thing that worried the man now was the fact that Gina knew of his dirty dealings. And if that rogue operative Alicia and her girlfriend kept digging like they were, they might just learn how he had built his wealth and how he continued to help fund The Company.

The old gentlemen might be ready for a new way of dealing with vampires, but they surely would not be ready for any illegal activities, no matter how much money those activities brought into their precious company.

Long ago, James had learned that you had to do what was necessary to get ahead. He was even blackballing his former best friend, Henry. But Henry was too stuck in the past to see the bright future that was ahead. Only he had the intellect to see into the future and what it would bring.

One day, the world would know about the efforts of The Company, and he would be even more rich and famous. After all, the world loved conquering heroes. And was not he just a mere hero in all the fighting that was going on?

A knock on his door interrupted his thoughts. "Come in."

The tall older woman that had been wearing a name badge that said Ester walked in slowly. "I have news."

James looked at the woman. "Not of the good, I take it."

She shook her head. "I tried to get the redhead like you asked, but that other woman somehow realized what I was doing or something. She came after me, and I had to run to get away."

"This is very disappointing." He took several steps toward the woman. "This is very disappointing indeed." Finally, he was face to face with the older woman. "You don't know me very well, but I don't take to disappointment. Not one bit."

"I can find them." She backed up a couple of steps. "I will find them and bring them both here. I won't fail you this time."

James' face became unreadable. "I suggest that you hurry. You won't be in my good graces for much longer unless you do. I've been meaning to make a statement. I could always start with you if you continue to not carry out my orders."

"Yes, sir." The woman quickly was at the door. "I won't fail you again." She tore open the door and slammed it shut.

Now James was smiling from ear to ear. "I think it is time to make a statement. Maybe I'll have to make a phone call." His phone rang at that very moment. "Hello?"

"Are you alone?" Kirk asked.

"I am now." James smiled. He knew why the man was calling. He had put on quite the show for the other top men, but James knew that the man was on the same page he was. "Is everything still going as planned?"

"Except for the fiasco that you have going for yourself." Kirk sighed heavily. "We have too much to lose if you continue to let those renegades run loose. Have you gotten any closer at all in ending all those questions those two are continually asking?"

"I may have found a way." James sounded annoyed. "I know very well how much is at stake. After all, you are the one that trained me. You let me in on the secrets that others still do not know about. I will do anything for The Company."

"That's good to know." Kirk cleared his throat. "It does make you wonder what the others are really thinking. The numbers don't add up if you look at them."

"I know." James began pacing. This phone call was not what he had expected. And it definitely was not what he wanted. All he wanted to do was to continue business as usual. No matter what the others thought that meant. "I will take care of things from this end. You make sure the others don't start digging around. That could be just as problematic."

"You handle your end. I'll handle mine." Kirk sighed. "And, James, do be careful. You are expendable. You do realize that."

The phone went dead at that very moment. James shuddered. He knew very well what Kirk was capable of. This was going to be an interesting few days. If he could not get the two lesbians to stop their inquiries, he would surely end up pushing up daisies.

Gina slowly but surely made her way through the sewers. If she was going to prove that Alicia was only after Andrea because of her work, it would take a special connection she had made. The thought of having to deal with the connection made her growl low in her throat.

Some past experiences had not been so pleasant. But to help out her Andrea was what was important. Gina would never admit it to anyone, including herself, but she was in love with the woman. In all her six hundred and twenty-two years, she had never felt like she did toward this woman. But there could never be anything between a vampire and a human.

Finally, she came up under the sewer for the street of Waverly. There was a little bookstore that not many people knew about. It was called "Mountain Books and Gifts." It was not your typical bookstore.

When Gina finally made her way in through the back entrance, the smell of incense greeted her immediately. There were many candles and very pretty crystals of varying sizes and colors. She knew that each of the candles and crystals had a special meaning. There were also books on astrology, meditation, and the art of witchcraft.

Standing behind the counter was a very tall woman with blonde hair down to the floor. She was in her early twenties. She wore a tan sun dress. Around her neck, she wore several pink crystals. Her smile was truly radiant.

Gina could not hold back the smile she always got when she saw the woman. She was one of the few people that knew the real face of the woman. Right now, she was probably wearing some black leather pantsuit. If her hair was its usual style, it would be spiked up, about six inches. The first color would be red, followed by pink and then purple. The woman also wore two nose rings and had her tongue pierced. But the glamour well-hid what was beneath.

The woman finally looked up. She sighed heavily as she saw who it was that had entered her establishment. With her head vigorously shaking, she asked, "What is it that you want now, Gina? I thought we had a deal that you wouldn't bother me anymore. Or have you forgotten?"

Quickly, Gina made her way to the counter. "I have not forgotten. But I have a serious problem. And only you know of the art of witchcraft. You are the only one that can help me, dear Susanna."

Susanna cringed at the name. "I hate it when you call me by my real name." She sighed again. "You know, I do have a coven. There are other witches out there besides me."

"Yes, but who is more powerful than you?" Gina smiled at the blonde. "Besides, you know who I am. The others would not take well with dealing with someone like me."

"You mean, someone that could drain their blood in two seconds?" Susanna walked over to the end of the counter. "Gee, I wonder why they wouldn't want to deal with you."

"Look, the sooner I get what I came for, the sooner I leave, and you won't have to deal with me." Gina came over and stepped in her path. "Hopefully, ever again."

"Don't threaten me, Gina." Susanna looked directly into the dark-haired vampire's eyes. "We both know that I am protected. That you and your kind can't harm me."

"Yes, but I know of others that might." Gina held her gaze steadily on the other woman.

Susanna shrugged. "Whatever. Let's just get this over with."

"Thank you." Susanna looked at her in surprise. Gina was not one for pleasantries of any kind. "I need to know if someone is telling the truth. Or at the very least, if I can trust this person. It is imperative that I know."

"It always is." Susanna stood thinking for a few minutes. "I assume that you would like to avoid contact?" Gina nodded. "I thought as much. You never can do things the easy way, can you?" She turned on her heels and headed toward the back room. Gina quickly followed. "You know, I don't let people back here."

"As you would be so quick to point out, I'm not really a person." Susanna shot her a look. "I just don't want to be seen here, that's all. I'll stay here in the corner."

91

Again, a look of surprise came across the witch. Gina was never considerate of others. She only wanted what was best for her. "This should do it." Susanna took a thick book off a shelf. "Even you can perform the spell. It's not really something that requires experience."

"You can provide me with the ingredients I will need?" Gina looked at the book after Susanna handed it to her.

"Well, this is sorta a magic store." She headed back to the front counter. "Although most just call it a new age store." She shrugged as she bent down and unlocked the back of the counter. After taking out several jars and putting them in a bag, she said, "This should be all you need. I hate to say this, but call me if you have any problems."

Gina nodded. "Thank you." She quickly made her way to the back door she had come in.

"If you keep up this attitude," Gina quickly turned to face her, "I might not be so hesitant to help you in the future."

Gina smiled and nodded as she left the store. Before the rays of the sun could catch her, she had lowered herself into the sewer below. She quickly headed for her lair. It was time to see if she could really trust that redhead. Especially since it would mean entrusting her with Andrea's life.

Alicia and Andrea were now in a car, driving west on West Saginaw Street. They were headed to the Red Roof Inn. They had a great time at Trippers. But it was now time to get back to business. After all, there were still people out to get them.

Andrea kept staring in the rearview mirror. A little white Ford Escort kept catching her eye. The detective in her was sending her signals. "I think we're being followed."

Alicia looked at her from concentrating on driving. "Which car?" She did not even ask if she were sure. The redhead already trusted her girlfriend's instincts.

"I think the white Ford Escort, four cars directly behind us." Andrea kept her eyes on the mirror. "Should we do a little experimenting?"

After raising her eyebrows, Alicia smiled at the look Andrea shot her. "I know what you meant. If we are being followed, we can't go to the hotel. At least not yet, anyway. You keep an eye on the car. I'll try out some of my fancy driving they taught me at The Company."

Alicia quickly moved into the left lane. Andrea watched as the white Ford did the same. "So far, they are sticking to us." Alicia quickly pulled into the left turn lane. Again, the car followed suit. "Two for two."

Nodding, Alicia waited for the light to turn green. She stepped quickly on the accelerator as soon as it did. The tires squealed, she took off so fast. "Hold on." They were now cruising down Creyts Road at about seventy miles an hour. Alicia kept weaving in and out of traffic. "Are they still behind us?"

Andrea smiled. The white car had been cut off at the light to Michigan Avenue. "You lost them, baby. You can slow down so that we don't get a ticket."

"Right." Alicia quickly returned to the speed limit of forty-five miles per hour. "So you want to cruise around town a little longer or do you think its safe to head for the hotel?"

"Hotel." Andrea looked over at her girlfriend. "That fancy driving of yours made me a little nauseous." She smiled at the look Alicia shot her. "Just teasing." She checked the rearview mirror again. "Seriously, though, if we hurry, we can make it to the hotel and park in back."

Nodding, Alicia made a left on St. Joe Highway. "It will take just a couple to get there. Then we can be all alone."

"We're all alone now." Andrea smiled. It was weird how she felt so comfortable around this other woman. She felt she could say or do anything. It was a feeling she had not had since her father was alive. Her face got a sad look at the thought of him.

"What's the matter?" They were already turning back on West Saginaw. "You seem sad all of a sudden."

"Just was thinking how comfortable and happy you make me." Andrea shrugged.

"And that makes you sad?" Alicia smiled.

"Well, I haven't felt this way since my dad was alive." Her eyes grew even sadder. "And that seems to have been an illusion. It wasn't real. Is this?"

Alicia reached over and took her hand. "Trust me when I say that it is real. I'm not hiding anything else from you. I'm sorry I did in the first place. But if I hadn't, who knows if we would have ever met."

Andrea finally smiled. "I do know that. It's just hard for me to truly trust people. But I do want to trust you. If you are hiding anything from me, tell me now. I will understand."

"If there was something to tell, I would." She squeezed Andrea's hand. "I think we need to talk. About what's going on and our past."

Henry crept down in the bushes outside the offices that he once was such a big part of. But thanks to his old friend, James, he was not even allowed access. It was frustrating, to say the very least.

The vibe that Henry got was that James was hiding something, more than the past criminal activities that he was well aware of and was actually a part of as well. There was something more. Henry could sense that James was going to try to take The Company in a whole new direction. Somewhere the founding fathers never would have wanted to go.

Not that it really mattered anymore. He knew now that there was no way for him to ever be included again. Once you were blacklisted, there was no returning to the A-list. That was what he had warned Alicia of. And that was something that he would never forgive James or Gina for. They had both helped to put him on the damn blacklist.

Gina. She had the largest part in his downfall. If he was not still trying to get the revenge that should so rightfully be his by now, he may still be in league with The Company now.

It did not really matter anymore. What was done, was done. There was no way that he could ever return to the fold. But he could still learn what was going on. If he had that knowledge, he could possibly use it to his advantage. Maybe he could even salvage some of the relationship he used to have with his stepdaughter. Not that they had ever really been close.

He pinned himself against the wall when he heard voices coming from around the corner of the building. One of them was definitely James'. He could not quite place the second one.

"We have to deal with all of them at the same time." James' booming voice carried so well. "I think we need to bring this all to a head, somehow. The longer it continues, the more that they are likely to find out. And that would not be a good thing for any of us."

"But we're not sure where any of them are at the moment." The voice was male and sounded youthful. Henry still was unsure who the strange man was.

James continued. "I know at least how to get a hold of the two lesbians. But the vampire and the renegade, now that's a different matter. I want as many men available tracking down the other two."

"But the two women?"

"Leave the women to me." James' voice was so assured. "I know exactly how to attract them. Just get the others on tracking down the rest."

"Yes, sir."

Henry crouched down as the two turned the corner. They stopped talking. He watched them for a few minutes. The renegade, he knew was himself. He chuckled. It was interesting to hear himself called what he had basically labeled his stepdaughter. At least he now knew that they were indeed after him. He would have to be extra careful.

Unfortunately, they did not know where the vampire was, either. That was the main reason he had ventured to his former employers. If they had known, he could have taken matters into his own hands. Eliminating her was still his top priority in all that was now going on.

And what was it that James knew or had that would make Alicia and Andrea surrender themselves? He knew his stepdaughter well. She would not give up without a fight. And what he knew of her girlfriend, she was no pushover, either.

He heard two car doors shut. The sound of two separate engines startled him. James and whoever he was with were going their separate ways. This could very well be his chance. He jumped up and hurried to his car. If he was fast enough, he might be able to follow his former friend. And then, maybe he could get the revenge he had sought for so many years.

Gina stared at the mixture she had created. She had done it precisely how the book had told her. Yet, there appeared to be no results. That could mean one of two things. Either she had royally screwed up or Alicia could indeed be trusted.

A growl ran through her throat as she knew the answer to the question. At least her Andrea was safe from the redhead. And that meant that she really did have an ally. That was of little comfort to her at the moment.

But that also made her think about how easy it would be for Andrea to now turn her back. If she had somebody else that she could trust, she may not be so inclined as before to believe in the vampire again.

She slammed the bowl down hard, shattering the pottery on the cement of the lair floor. It could not have been true that Alicia could not be trusted. That would have made things easier and simpler. Now, things were very complicated. But then, life always seemed to be complicated.

There was also the thought that she had no clue as to where Andrea had herself hidden. Hopefully, it was some place safe. And there was James and Henry running around. Those two could easily be trouble for them all.

If only Gina had not fallen into James' sick scheme all those years ago. She had been desperate for money all those years ago. It used to be that money was not a big deal for her. But in these modern times, money meant almost everything. Even to a thing that required only blood to survive.

But to most vampires, money meant very little. That was why when James approached her about using some of her fellow creatures of the night to traffic drugs, she had at first resisted. They would not be bought by money or trinkets or such. She knew what they craved. And she knew that almost all of them would do anything to fix that craving.

It had been her idea to start paying them in blood. But she knew that they would not be satisfied with animal blood like she had long ago become accustomed to. No, these vampires had no conscience. After all, no vampire had a soul. Not once they had died. Their soul was released, and an empty shell remained.

She was one of the lucky ones that had kept a conscience. Most only walked around answering to the bloodlust that was a part of them all. Even she had such a bloodlust. But unlike the other walking dead, she knew how to control it.

James had jumped at the idea of paying the vampire lackeys with human blood. And since the Red Cross was a voluntary thing, no one was really getting hurt. And it made them both quite rich.

Gina knew that he had used part of his money to fund The Company. It was ironic that the people that wanted her death, and those like her, were being helped by a vampire.

Andrea's father had found out about the theft of blood and who was behind it. He also learned about why they had stolen the blood. The man had seen his opportunity to get in on the cash bandwagon. But the man had become too greedy. And James had seen fit to call out the enforcers.

If she had not learned what James had done, she never would have been able to save Andrea that day nearly twenty years ago. But she had not been able to save Henry's son.

That was another story. He had come across the vampires selling drugs. He had wanted in. The only way was to become one of them. And once he did, he became too greedy. Gina had to take care of him.

And now, it was all about to come out. The illegal activities she had been a part of, The Company's dirty dealings, and Andrea's father also becoming a cop on the take. It was going to end badly. Gina could see that now. In her unbeating heart, she was glad that at least Andrea had someone she could trust. Gina was truly alone.

Andrea looked up as there was a knock on the door. Quickly, she made her way over and looked out the peephole. The red hair gave away instantly who it was. She unlatched the chain and let Alicia in. "Took you long enough." She quickly shut the door and latched the chain.

Alicia shrugged as she made her way over to the small dining room table in the next room. She set down the bag of groceries she had gotten. "Well, it's better than take out, and we really don't want to draw attention by ordering room service."

Andrea could not help but stare at the other woman. They had not really talked about anything as of yet. And she had a feeling that the redhead was distancing herself. It was the hint that she still was not sure that she could trust the other woman that was driving the wedge between them.

A huge sigh escaped the sandy blonde. Alicia noticed and stopped putting the food away. She made her way to stand in front of the other woman. Both women stared a moment, searching each other to see if there was something they could see in the other's face. But there was just a long period of silence.

It was Andrea that finally broke the tension between them. She pulled the redhead into a tight embrace. "I'm sorry if it sounded like I was doubting you."

Alicia did not break the embrace. She held on tight as well. "But you were doubting me. We may not have known each other long, but I could tell that it was me you were doubting and not this whole situation."

Finally, Andrea pulled back a little so that she could look her in the eyes. "I know. I was doubting you. Even when every fiber of my being tells me that you are the one thing in this world that I can trust and hold onto, I still let my insecurities get the better of me."

"You've never had to trust anyone before, have you?" Alicia raised her eyebrows at the thought.

"Only Gina." Now Andrea pulled out of the embrace and started to play with the remaining groceries. Alicia came up from behind and wrapped her arms around her. "And look how well that has turned out so far."

"But you still trust me. And…" Alicia draped her head on Andrea's shoulder.

"Still love you?" Andrea turned around and faced her. "Yes. To both. I may get like this every once in a while. And I'm sorry for that. It's just a hard habit to break. Not feeling you can trust anybody."

"Listen. I don't know why you feel the way you do." Alicia smiled shyly. "We've only talked a little about the other's pasts. Things have happened to both of us. Together, we can get through anything."

"Including the fact that my father was into illegal activities of some kind, Gina really is the one that killed your stepbrother, and I think that Gina was into stealing blood almost twenty years ago." Andrea smiled at the look on Alicia's face.

"Well. The old-fashioned method really came through." Alicia took the other woman's hand. "You really do know your way around even without technology."

"It was all there in black and white." Andrea sighed. "If this is all true, I wonder if Gina was into the illegal stuff that my father was. That would explain why she wouldn't want me finding out."

"Oh, my findings." Alicia smiled. "I got into the coroner's office. My stepbrother's body was taken there, and there were puncture wounds on the neck. But the body somehow vanished during the night. There was no report of breaking and entering. It just disappeared."

"Or maybe it got up and walked away." Andrea took in the look on her girlfriend's face. "I'm not saying it's a certainty, but that would explain the body just simply disappearing and the puncture wounds. And if he were a vampire, then maybe Gina did what she does. She gets rid of those that don't follow their consciences."

"That would be a happier scenario than what Daddy dearest has been trying to portray." Alicia began pacing. "And I know my stepfather. I know that even if he had all the proof in the world, he wouldn't believe that Frederick would choose to go to the bad side."

"Instead, he would continue to blame Gina." Andrea nodded. "And she wouldn't give up on the fact that somebody was out to get her. She may even try to take matters into her own hands."

"Even if this is all true, it really doesn't explain why The Company would be so hot to get to us. Illegal activity by a cop twenty years ago, possibly a vampire killing another vampire, and stolen blood? It really doesn't add up." Alicia stopped pacing and stared at Andrea.

"Maybe there's somebody else. Somebody that was in on the illegal activity." Andrea's eyes lit up. "Maybe somebody fairly high up at The Company is involved in all of this and doesn't want us to expose him."

Alicia's eyes lit up as well. "That would definitely explain why they would be going after us like we are common criminals on the run. We aren't the ones that did anything wrong. Maybe we've just stumbled onto somebody else."

The two slowly came closer to each other. "And because they think we have enough pieces of the puzzle, we've become a serious liability. They can't let us go. They will do anything and anything to keep our mouths shut."

The two stood inches away. "And because the two of us are so smart and work so well with each other, they knew it wouldn't be long before we would put two and two together." Alicia smiled.

They stared at each other for a moment. Both swooped in at the same time. Their lips touched, first gently, then more and more aggressively. Both of their breathing began to get ragged. Slowly, Andrea slipped her brown leather jacket off. Alicia did the same with her black wool coat.

They broke a part for another minute catching their breaths. Then their lips were meeting again. Andrea's hands found the front of Alicia's shirt. Slowly and with purpose, she began unbuttoning the soft white shirt. Andrea was about to slip it off when there was a soft chirping from the pocket of her leather jacket.

"Damn!" Andrea broke away from the moment breathing heavily. The chirping continued annoyingly. "Just when it was getting too hot to handle." She reached into her jacket and pulled out the offending cell phone.

"Don't answer it." Alicia quickly came up and stood behind her. She began playing with the button of Andrea's black jeans.

"As much as I'd love to continue this, only two people know this number." She put her hand on Alicia's. "It could be Gina trying to get to me or Adam may very well be in danger."

"You'd better answer it." The phone rang for the sixth time. "We can always finish this later."

"I promise we will." Finally, she flipped open the phone. "Hello?"

"Miss Freemont, I was beginning to think you weren't going to take such an important phone call." The deep voice sent chills up and down her spine.

"Who is this?" Andrea was going to ask how they had gotten her cell phone number, but in her heart, she already knew. And her heart was afraid for Adam.

"Let's just say I'm someone that holds something you actually care about. The boy is just so innocent, isn't he?"

"What have you done to Adam?" Alicia stepped closer at the mention of his name. "Don't hurt him."

"My dear, we have no intention of hurting him." The voice seemed to be getting a great deal of pleasure out of the conversation. "But we will if you don't cooperate with us. We want you and your girlfriend to meet us. And bring that damn vampire with you."

"I can't guarantee the vampire." Her mind began racing with all the possible ways that this could end and none of them were pleasant. "But you've got me and her."

"That will do for now." There was a muffled sound. The voice was talking to somebody else for a moment. "We have set up a time and place. If at least the two of you do not show, we will begin hurting the boy. We can be very unpleasant. Oh, and bring any of the notes that you gathered at the library and anything else in your private files.

Bring them to the private dining room of Chez Pierre. We won't be disturbed that way. Ten tomorrow morning. Or we begin having fun with the boy."

There was a click and the phone went dead. Andrea slammed the phone shut. "Damn! I can't believe this." She looked up at the redhead. "I really think they are going to kill us. And Adam as well, no matter what."

Henry could not believe his ears. He was standing outside a local grocery store where James had stopped. James did not stop to buy a gallon of milk and a loaf of bread. Instead, he had used their payphones to make a phone call. And he had somebody with him. Henry did not recognize the man.

And the son of a bitch was threatening people's lives, including his stepdaughter's. Was this really the direction The Company was headed? And if it was, there was no way that Henry could ever go back.

Henry had done some things in his time that would not necessarily be considered ethical but to actually take innocent lives was different. That was one thing that he would never do, at least not human lives.

He slipped into the sudden throng of people rushing out of the store. As fast as he could, he made it to his car. Barely watching where he was going, he squealed out of the parking lot. Not really headed anywhere, he pulled out his cell phone. He needed an ally. Or at least somebody that still had some clout and would give him a little bit of benefit of the doubt.

It was not long until he was talking to his friend Kirk. Kirk had long ago recruited Henry. They were still very close. And hopefully he still valued Henry's opinion.

"Hello?" The voice sounded concerned on the other end.

"Kirk, is there something wrong?" Henry knew his friend well enough to know the answer to that question.

"What in the devil are you doing calling me?" There was no hiding the annoyance in his voice.

"I thought you'd like to know what your new leader was up to. But if you'd rather stay in the dark, that's up to you."

There was a huge sigh from the other end of the line. "It's just that we've been told that you are now a renegade. You are aligning yourself with your stepdaughter and that vampire."

"Hell no!" Henry's breathing began to pickup. "Maybe Alicia isn't as wrong as I originally thought she was. But the vampire still needs to be taken care of. Any way necessary."

"That's been your problem, Henry. You can't seem to back off when it's as personal as it is for you." Kirk cleared his throat. "You could have let others handle things for you. But instead, you've now gotten in over your head."

"And what about James?" Henry laughed. "Has he free reign in all of this? And I do mean free."

"What in the devil are you talking about?"

Henry sighed. "That's why I called you. Believe me or not but I just heard your new leader order the torture and possible death of a human. Several humans in fact. I'm just wondering how long The Company has allowed such things to go on. Or have we all been lending a blind eye when it comes to James and some of the others in the organization?"

"You can't be serious!" Kirk's voice could not contain his anger. "Henry, are you really that far gone that you would say such things about your former friend?"

"I'm beginning to believe that he was never my friend." Henry took a deep breath, trying to gather his thoughts. "You've known me since I was a young man. You were the one that recruited me for the job in the first place. I am all that you taught me and more. I didn't want to believe it either, but I've heard with my own ears. James is out of control. And there are other things you should know about him. Things he's done over the years."

"What are you talking about?"

"Just get back here. Before ten tomorrow if you can. That's when he's set the trap for Alicia and her girlfriend. And for Gina." Henry swerved to avoid a slow-moving vehicle. "If you won't believe me, at least come and find out for yourself. The meeting is at Chez Pierre's."

He hung up his cell phone and tossed it onto the seat next to him. It appeared that Henry was running out of options. If he did not think of something before tomorrow, it was very likely the last day that his stepdaughter would be alive.

Gina paced in her lair. For some reason, she felt that time was slipping away from her. She had eternal life but felt that there was not enough time.

She so wanted to be out there looking for Andrea, or even better yet, James or Henry. If she could find those two, she could protect her charge without her even knowing. Andrea must be kept safe at all costs. And she must never know that her father was involved in the illegal activities.

As was her habit, a growl formed deep in her throat. It was the predator in her coming out whenever she got frustrated or angry. It had been happening a lot the past few days. There was a lot going on that she did not like.

The chirping of her cell phone made her growl even deeper. It had disturbed her thoughts. Her mind raced a little before she answered the ringing phone. There were only two people that knew of her number. And one of them was dead. She could not help but hope that it was she.

"Hello?" Her deep steady voice covered the anticipation and fear she was feeling.

"It's Andrea." This voice was showing the distance that the owner felt. Still unsure whether or not she could trust the vampire, she knew in her heart that she would need a powerful ally when she faced the unknown.

"You are still speaking to me. This is a pleasant surprise." Gina was masking the great relief she felt. Her tone remained as even as she could make it.

"Only because I know I will need muscle tomorrow. And you are still the strongest person I know." She hesitated for a moment. "Besides, you were invited, too."

"Invited?" A little bit of surprise managed to make it into the dark-haired vampire's voice.

"There is a trap that has been setup for tomorrow at ten in the private dining room of Chez Pierre." Her voice was telling the fear she felt. "They've got Adam and have requested that you, me, and Alicia attend this soiree. I told them that I may not be able to get you to come."

"And yet you call and invite me." Gina let that sink in for a moment before continuing. It was probably just the fear for the boy and the realization that she would surely be outgunned by whatever the opposition would have waiting for them. "I will come. I will defend you until the very end. No matter what you may now think of me."

"I've discovered some things about you." Andrea sighed. "Maybe they're true. Maybe they are just speculation on my part. When this is over, maybe then we can sit down and talk honestly about what happened twenty years ago. I'm not a child anymore, Gina. I realize that sometimes things happen that we are not proud of. We just have to get past them if we can."

Andrea was holding the door open. But what exactly was it that she had discovered about her past? Gina was unsure of what to think. Maybe her charge would be able to understand that she had let herself be fooled into taking the easy way out. Maybe. Or maybe she was just biding time and using Gina now that she so desperately needed her.

"I would like that very much. I fear we have a lot to talk about." Gina now sighed. "And perhaps we can learn to move on from the past."

"Perhaps. About tomorrow, I'm not really sure what to expect. All I know is that they have threatened to harm Adam if we do not show up." Andrea shook her head. "I can't and won't let that happen. He's one of the good people in this world."

"Along with your new love." Gina was not about to pull any punches. If there was a chance that the two of them could still be friends, she knew that she would have to accept the fact that Alicia was now a big part of her life. A bigger part than Gina ever was.

"Y-you know about Alicia and accept her?" The voice that came through was full of surprise.

"Of course." Gina laughed softly. "I, of course, did some checking on her. She has a good heart. I believe that she will only be good for you if you let her. And tomorrow, I vow to protect both of you with my eternal life."

"Wow!" Andrea was smiling on the other end, and Gina could hear the smile. "Thanks. I just wish that things could go back to the way they were for us. You have always been there for me as long as I can remember. But things have changed, and I'm not sure if we'll ever be able to get them back."

"There is time for that later." Gina's unbeating heart broke as she said, "You need to spend your time with the one that you love. Not to be negative, but these could be the last few hours that you spend together. Please enjoy them. I will try and find out what is to happen tomorrow. I think it is time that I paid Henry a surprise visit. And only to talk. I promise."

"Again, thank you. We plan on using the time to get a plan of our own together. We're coming in as armed as we can." Andrea laughed. "Just don't have that much of an arsenal at our disposal. We'll just do the best that we can until then."

"And in the meantime, I will continue to watch over you as always."

James practically towered over the five-foot dark-haired man with a gold stripe down the middle. They were standing outside the Elmwood Plaza Theaters. It was nearly 11 p.m., and they were discussing the next day's events.

"You have done well in tricking Gina into believing that, first, she could trust you. Second, convincing her that you were one of the ones that died in the warehouse fire." James had a huge grin on his face. "I always knew where your loyalties were, Ricky."

Now there was a huge smile on the vampire's face. "Gina still scares me, but if we can get rid of her, it would be my simple pleasure to put myself at risk."

Now James shook his head. "I still don't get the fear that you and the others have of this vampire. She is just like you, is she not?"

Ricky emphatically shook his head. "If you believe that, then you won't be able to face her and live. She has been around for more than six hundred years. In that time, she has studied the best defenses and offenses available. In addition, she has learned to adapt to the times."

"And it is that adaption that may very well be her undoing. At least with her so-called charge." James shrugged his shoulders. "But that's not our biggest goal, now is it. Our biggest goal is to rid the fair city of the vampire. She is too big of a threat for us to continue the actions that she so long ago thought that we had stopped."

"If she ever found out…" Ricky trailed off at the look that the dark-skinned man shot him.

"She once was part of the very thing that she now seeks to stop." He chuckled softly. "I find it ironic that she now crusades so hard against what we do. Speaking of what we do, do you have another wiser crew than the last one that was so easily taken out by the operatives?"

"In place and ready for the word." Ricky looked up at the tall man. "Are you really going to pay us with human blood?" It appeared that the vampire was actually salivating at the thought of human blood.

A disturbed look came across James' face. "Really. That is disgusting. But rest assured I have a way that they will all be fed, and it will be with human blood."

Ricky rubbed his hands together in anticipation. "I'm going to go and tell the others and prepare them for the big day tomorrow. Until then." Ricky turned to go.

"Uh, Ricky." The little vampire turned back. "Exactly how many of your friends should I expect at the party I'm throwing? I just need a guest count for the caters."

"Twenty, including me." He turned and quickly disappeared into the shadows of the night.

"Excellent."

Gina always seemed to know where the man was. It amazed her that it was still twenty years and the feud between the two of them continued, especially when he was so easy for her to find. Why had she not yet finished the feud?

Then her conscience gave her the answer. He was a human. His grief was still strong, even after all these years. And because she was something unnatural, it was easier for him to blame her and try to take out that grief on her.

She shrugged at the thought. If he should need someone to blame, it might as well be she. After all, it was one of the gangs that she had paid with human blood to deliver the drugs that had turned his son. Granted, it was not her fault that he had so easily been swayed by the large sums of money and prestige he saw. And he could have easily said no to becoming a vampire.

Although she had not been sure when she had accepted Hector's offer to turn her, she had been unsure of what to expect. If she had it to do all over again, she would refuse and let her short life live out in the way it was supposed to. The only good thing that remained in her life was Andrea. And she now belonged to another.

Henry was pacing back and forth in the Cozy Inn, a dive on Oakland Avenue. She could not tell if he was upset or just restless. Then a thought hit her. He could very well know about the upcoming events. That made things a lot more interesting than before. Perhaps if he did know, he would not be so quick to continue their feud. But this was Henry she was talking about. The only thing that he understood was revenge.

Doing the most unusual thing she had ever done, she knocked on the door to his room. She watched as he grabbed his chest. From his left pocket, he took a wooden stake. From his right pocket, he took a revolver. This was not going to be easy.

His eye about bulged out the little peephole as he looked out. He opened the door, leaving the chain latched. "You are the last thing I expected to see on my doorstep. What in the hell do you want?" Gina felt herself starting to growl. It took all her strength and restraint to stifle it. "You know about tomorrow; I know you do, Henry." His eyes widened a little. "I've come to ask that we work together. And not for me. It would never be for me. If I was dust blowing in the wind, it would not matter much. But if any of the three innocents are harmed, I would not like it very much at all."

Henry stared at her for a few minutes. "You are here looking for an ally in me?" Gina simply nodded in response. He burst out in a fit of laughter. "That's just so rich. You come to me when your charge is in trouble. Does she know this?" He hesitated. "Does Alicia know? Is she in danger as well?"

"You know your stepdaughter better than I do." Gina stared at him. "Do you think she would let innocent lives hang in the balance when she thought she may have a chance to put a stop to it? You tell me."

"Damn!" Henry answered loudly. "I'm not letting you in. Just know that I will be there, and I will do everything in my power to save my daughter. And if you get in my way, I will personally see that you are dust. Is that clear?"

Gina shrugged. "Just remember one thing, while they are in danger, we are on the same team. And I will fight to the death for both your daughter and my Andrea. And even you. But when the danger is over, all bets are off. Is that clear?" Both glared at each other before Henry slammed the door shut.

She stared for several minutes at the door. Gina knew that Henry would do anything in his power to right the perceived wrongs that had been committed against him. The ones by her and the ones that The Company had committed. It was going to be a long and painful day tomorrow.

It was closing in on one in the morning. The feeling that tomorrow was indeed her last day kept hanging over her. She watched the redhead sleeping so peacefully. She wanted nothing more than to get in bed with her and wrap her arms around the woman. But Andrea was also terrified.

One of the bad habits she had picked up over the years was not being able to sleep when something exciting or scary was going to happen. This was definitely one of those times. But she was not scared for herself or even Adam. No. She was more terrified at the thought of something happening to the woman sleeping in the bed.

Andrea resumed her pacing. She tried to walk as quietly as possible. Just because she was having difficulty sleeping was no reason that Alicia needed to be sleepy during whatever was to take place tomorrow.

And exactly what was it that was going to take place? Was it going to be talking about what they knew? That would be too easy and against the conversation of the phone call. No. She knew that it was going to end up being a big battle. She was actually going to have to be in a knock down fight.

It had been years since she had been in an actual fight. The last time was when she had said the wrong thing in the basement of Max's Bar and Grill. She had offended a hunday demon. Usually very mild and peaceful, she had found out that if you told them they were fun, it meant something else. All hell had broke loose, and she had barely escaped with a black eye and two cracked ribs.

As she turned to pace the other way, she almost ran into Alicia. She jumped back. "Whoa!"

"Sorry, hotty. Didn't mean to startle you." Alicia stood in a pink satin robe that hung loosely around her unclothed body. "Just was wondering why you weren't in bed with me or do I have to ask?"

Andrea shrugged. "Just never been able to sleep before something big going down. Been that way since I was little. Guess it's not about to change."

"Didn't I wear you out just a little earlier?" Alicia came and wrapped her arms around the sandy blonde. "You got dressed. What for?"

Andrea let out a little laugh and held on tight. "You are so wonderful. Where have you been all my life?"

"Working for people that lied to me every chance they got." Alicia felt Andrea shiver. "What's the matter, and don't tell me you were just turned on by me. I know the difference."

Andrea pulled back. "You are so different from me. You use humor in the face of danger. And I…"

"Become a stuck up tight ass?" Alicia smiled as Andrea frowned at her. "Sorry. I've always tried to use humor to lighten stressful times. But seriously, I think I understand where you're coming from. I've never really been in an actual battle before. The thought of you getting hurt is too much for me so I push it away and make a joke." She shrugged. "It's what I do."

"And I pace back and forth." The image of Alicia getting hurt flashed in her mind again. "I wish I could shut off my damn brain for two seconds. I keep seeing you in various positions." Alicia raised her eyebrows. "Covered with bruises and blood and not breathing."

Alicia nodded. "Listen. We're both scared. But remember that we both have Gina watching out for us. It's an added secret weapon. We'll be all right."

"Do you really think so?" Andrea sighed. "I'm sort of a pessimist, you know. I'm always looking on the bad side. That's why I'm still having trouble with the thought that you and I will be able to make it. I want you so badly."

"In every way?" Andrea answered with a very passionate kiss. "I guess so." Alicia smiled at her girlfriend. "I believe we were fated to be together. And if we were fated to be together, why would we be separated so quickly?" She pulled Andrea into another long and passionate kiss. "Let's go back to bed. Ten is so very far away. Maybe I can wear you out just a little, and you can actually get some sleep."

❖

Ricky and the other vampires he had gathered looked around the fancy dining room. In a few hours, it would prove to be the site of an historic battle. At least, he hoped it would be an historic battle. If he could rid himself of Gina, he could become the one that controlled Lansing, along with The Company and James, of course.

That would be the only catch. He would have to share the power. But at least they were on the same page as he. They had no conscience like Gina did, and they were human. There was nothing holding them back.

"Are you sure about this Ricky?" a female vampire asked. "I mean, we're going to piss Gina off royally if we don't win. That'll mean a lot of us not surviving to see another sunset."

Ricky smiled. "Don't be so negative. We've got the backing of one of the most powerful organizations in the world. We're not going to be in this alone. James promised me some of his best operatives as well. They'll make sure that we succeed."

A very large male vampire stepped forward. "We had better. I really don't want to have to deal with Gina. She'll be the toughest in a fight. Maybe we should go for her first, instead of the two women."

Shaking his head, Ricky said, "Are you guys getting scared on me now? That's not a good thing. We have the upper hand. They don't know that we'll be here and how many of us there are. Besides, we're vampires, and they're just women. I think we can handle them."

"What about Gina?" the large vampire asked more forcefully. "She's the best fighter of all of us. She knows more and has been around longer. Are you really so sure about her?"

A huge sigh escaped Ricky. "Listen. We have the upper hand. We have them outnumbered. We know what to expect. This is going to be easy. Just everybody chill. It won't be that long, and we'll be fighting."

"Very well said." All twenty vampires turned to see who had spoken. It was James. And he had an older black-haired woman with him. "Ricky is right. You have the upper hand. And I will have operatives surrounding the restaurant if you should somehow fail. If you should need reinforcements, they will be there for you. Just don't let me down, and you have nothing to worry about."

Ricky turned to the others. "We can do it. You guys just haven't faced a real battle in a long time. Remember the rewards. Money. Human blood. It all adds up to real goodness."

James turned to go. "And just think, if you fail, you'll be helping to fertilize the earth. How poetic." All twenty sets of eyes stared after him. "Speaking of failing." Before he did, he pushed the woman toward the pack of vampires. "Ester here was unable to complete a simple task for me. Would you please see to it that she is properly rewarded?" He turned to go. He paused for a moment again. "Just remember, I can reward you in similar ways."

Gina watched the scene unfold before her. She could not believe that Ricky was still alive, more or less. And more, he was setting her up. This was making her very cranky which was very bad for all those vampires inside.

It gave her extra incentive. Not that she really needed any. There was Andrea to protect. There would always be Andrea to protect. That was a given.

Her vampire senses knew that the sun was only minutes away from appearing. She knew that she had to find cover. It would have to be close to the restaurant. She was not about to fail in this mission. That would mean that Andrea would die.

Even if it meant she somehow did not survive, she would not let down her charge. She had been too late to save her father. And now Andrea's life was hanging in the balance again. Another thought crossed her mind. Where was Adam?

Chills went up and down her spine as she feared she knew the answer to that question. She walked around to the back of Chez Pierre's. There was a service entrance. Using her vampire strength, she twisted the knob until it turned. Slowly, she made her way through the back entrance.

Gina could hear the bustling of the workers preparing for the start of their day. This was another added complication. There would be innocent people in the line of fire, never a good thing when one was battling for one's life or existence.

A door marked "basement entrance" caught her eye. She slowly made her way down into the darkness, letting her vampire eyes adjust. Just as she reached the bottom of the steps, a very familiar scent caught her attention.

As quickly as she could, she followed the scent like a blood hound. Which was ironic because that was the scent she was following. Blood. And there was a lot of it. Gina nearly slipped in something wet and slippery. She bent down to examine what had nearly made her fall. A huge growl roared from her throat. It was a huge puddle of blood.

She slowly stood. Slowly, she kept going forward. Finally, she made it to the back wall of the basement. There was something hanging in the corner. Still slowly so that she did not slip and fall, she made her way over to what had caught her attention.

Another growl grew in her throat. Tied and gagged, Adam hung staring into space. His breathing was very shallow. His body was covered in tiny cuts. His face was nothing but a huge bruise. If she did not act fast, he would surely die.

As carefully as she could, she got Adam down from the restraints. With every touch, he moaned softly. She untied his hands from behind his back and laid him gently on the floor. She untied his feet that also had been bound. Finally, she took the gag out of his mouth.

From past experience, she could tell that he needed blood and quickly. Two puncture wounds on his neck caught her eye. Quietly, she asked, "They didn't make you drink their blood, did they?" She dearly hoped not. If she could get him to a hospital, he would have a chance at surviving. But if he had drank…

Adam managed to slowly shake his head. He began coughing and spitting up blood. She could see the pain surging throughout his body. Suddenly, there was more blood on the floor.

She gently rolled him over. They had put in a tube. When she had moved him, the tube had opened up causing more blood to come out.

"Damn!" She put her hand over the end of the tube. Looking around, she found a pile of tablecloths. She ripped them in half and wrapped his entire body. "This is going to be painful for you, but I've got to get you to the hospital. I'm sorry."

Before he could acknowledge her in any way, she had him cradled in her arms. To her relief, there was a huge grate that lead to the sewers. As carefully and quickly as she could, she lowered herself and him down.

The path to the hospital was very familiar to her. She had it mapped out in her mind from any location in the city. That had been done just in case it had ever been Andrea she needed to save. With each step she took, a soft moan escaped her handful.

Fortunately, it was only five blocks to the nearest hospital. The sewer lead to the kitchen. Forcing the grate open with a bang, she set Adam down gently. She quickly covered the opening back up. Making sure that no one was coming at the sound, she again picked up Adam.

It was not long before she found a gurney. She set him on it and found the emergency room doors. Instead of going in with him, she sent the gurney gently through the opening. Knowing that it would not be long before somebody discovered him, she took off back to the sewer entrance. She needed to get back to her hiding place. And she needed to tell Andrea what The Company was really capable of.

Henry slammed his cell phone shut. It was official. He was definitely a renegade now. Not even his friend Kirk would take his phone calls. And Kirk had not listened to him. The man was still deluding himself in Tokyo.

Pacing back and forth, Henry was not sure what he was to do. His life work was slipping away from him. He could very easily keep blaming Gina and James. But it was really his fault that all of this was happening.

If he had his eyes open, he might have seen all the dirty dealings that James was involved in. It was true that he himself had taken part in a couple. But those had been traps to try and rid himself of that vile vampire.

He stopped and put his head in his hands. The hour was drawing nearer. He looked around at his surroundings. The motel was a dive. The rug had cigarette burns. The wallpaper was covered with greasy stains. And he did not even want to think about the sheets on the bed and what people had done in them.

How had his life sunk from staying at five star hotels to this? Again, if he were honest with himself, he knew. It was all his fault. A life of revenge had cost him all the things that he had held dear.

Even before she had taken his son's life, he had been plagued by the dark-haired vampire. His efforts to rid himself of her were still there. Just not quite as intense as they became once she had put an end to his son.

If he could put an end to his vendetta, he could make up for a lot of things that he had done over the years. His one wish was to open the eyes of those higher ups that now looked so far down on him. They needed to know what was going on in their precious organization if they did not already know.

But it was just so hard trying to let go of the anger and pain he had been clinging to for the past twenty plus years. Gina had vexed him so many times. And she was the one that had ultimately cost him his son.

But there was his stepdaughter and the other innocents to think about. He was sure that James would put operatives in place just in case any of the vampire lackeys he was sure to have failed. Also, there were the workers of Chez Pierre. And that would mean that many more people that could easily get hurt. This was becoming so complicated and intense. And there was not a solution he could see.

He would just have to be prepared for everything and anything. And if the opportunity presented itself, he would kill his foe. After all the people were safe, he would take her out, once and for all.

Andrea sat at the little breakfast nook between the kitchen and the living room of the hotel room. She watched as Alicia was still sleeping. A smile made it to her face. The woman really could sleep anytime, even before a fight for their lives.

A beep came from the coffee maker. She pulled out two cups and poured herself and Alicia one. Hearing a muffled sound, she turned to see Alicia stretching. Her red hair was still beautifully messed up. The sheet concealed her beautiful body.

"Morning," Andrea said and quickly made her way to the bed. "You certainly are a sound sleeper." She handed her girlfriend one of the coffees.

"Not necessarily a good thing. After all, a good operative is always alert." She gladly took the cup of coffee. "Thanks." The curtains were covering the window, but she could see the sun trying to peak around the edges. "What time is it? Or more accurately, how long do we have before we definitely kick some major league ass?"

"There's that optimist in you." Andrea shrugged at the look. "Just noticing how different we are in some ways, that's all. And it's eight. We don't have long to get stocked up and prepare for the major ass kicking. Hopefully not our own."

"Wow!" Alicia quickly stood, letting the sheet drop off her and expose her radiant body. "I guess we'd better get moving."

Andrea stood quickly and pulled her into a quick kiss. "Sorry. Just couldn't resist, you look so damn sexy."

Alicia smiled. "There'll be lots of time for that later. I'd rather be with you than possibly getting hurt any day. But for now, we just have to do what we can."

"Have you actually ever battled vampires or demons before?" Andrea walked back to the breakfast nook. She sat down and watched her girlfriend get dressed.

"You think that The Company would employ using those that they are supposed to be eliminating?" She held up a hand. "Stupid question after what we've been through the past few days. I'd say that they'd do anything and anything necessary to cover their asses. Do you really think that we have that much on them that we are that much of a threat?"

"All that matters is that they think so." Andrea shrugged. "I've had some big battles over the years with the undead and some of their compatriots. We will need lots of weapons. Only problem, I don't think it's safe to go to the office or to either of our apartments at the moment. Any other ideas?"

Alicia shook her head. "Nada. Wish we would have stocked up more before we ran for our lives. But gee, we really didn't have a whole lot of time to think, now did we?"

Andrea could not help but laugh. This woman was so different and yet was exactly what she needed in her life. Her thoughts were interrupted by her cell phone. "Wonder if they're changing the plans." She took her phone out of her jacket pocket. "Hello?"

"It's Gina." The familiar voice almost sounded scared. That caught Andrea's attention right away. "I found Adam. I believe he will be all right. Hopefully, I got him to St. Lawrence in time."

Andrea shuddered. "It was that bad?"

"He lost a lot of blood. They cut him to torture him and fed off from him as well. There was a trap. I moved the boy and a tube opened up causing more blood to drain even more quickly." There was that oh so familiar growl in her throat. "You've got twenty vampires waiting for you. And you'll have human company as well. I'm on my way back to Chez Pierre. I'll be watching out for both of you. Oh, and Henry promised he would be there as well."

Andrea's face was a little pale at the description of Adam. Her eyes widened when she heard Henry was also going to show. "You mean, Henry's going to help us out?" Alicia quickly stood by her lover.

"He promised to put aside our differences at least until the fight is over." Gina sighed. "He still may come after me. I am not so sure."

"Listen, gotta favor to ask." Andrea hesitated. "We seem to be really lacking on the weapons department. I still have my gun, but nothing to really fight the vampires. Any way you could come up with something to help us out?"

"Go to my lair." Gina hesitated. "There are plenty of weapons there. And hurry. Time is growing short."

"Thanks." Before she hung up, she managed to get out, "I appreciate you watching out for me." She slammed the phone shut.

"Well, what was that about my stepfather?" Alicia sat next to her at the breakfast nook.

"The condensed version. We have twenty vamps waiting for us, who knows how many operatives, and your stepfather has agreed to help." Andrea took another sip of her coffee.

"Wow!" Alicia took Andrea's hand. "You know I'm big on the jokes and all, but I'm really scared. And I mean really scared. I never had to actually fight a vampire before with the exception of that little conflict we had in my apartment."

"Well, I guess you'd better stick by my side." Andrea stood up. "We'd better get going. I want to get to Gina's so that we have plenty of time to get to the battle."

"Gina's?" Alicia questioned.

"Forgot that in my summary." Andrea smiled. "She has lots of weapons in her lair. In the sewers." Andrea could not help but laugh at the look of disgust on Alicia's face. "It's not so bad if you hold your nose and try not to breathe while you're down there. Really."

"I'll do anything if it means saving your sexy ass." Alicia smiled. "Even sinking to the depths of the sewer."

Gina kept her eyes and ears open. There was much movement in the private dining room. But she knew. She had always been able to sense others of her kind. That was how she had found Andrea all those years ago.

She shook her head at the thought of Andrea. The thought of her made her head spin. This woman was someone she had protected for so long. But now, she no longer needed protection. Andrea was embracing life. The only thing she needed was for somebody to stand by her when things got bad. And she had Alicia for that.

The faintest of sounds caught her attention. The familiar scent in the air made her smile. "Thank you for coming, Henry."

Henry stepped out of the shadows. Both were in the hallway leading to the private dining room. "You've got to have a better hiding place than this."

Gina shrugged. "As soon as I can get inside. Currently, there are twenty vampires inside. Are there any operatives outside?"

Henry nodded. "The last count, thirty. But they will not enter the battle unless things go badly in here. James would rather sacrifice his vampire lackeys than actually put humans at any real risk."

"I know." Gina half smiled at the man. "He tried with me many times. But I'm not like other vampires, now am I?"

Henry laughed softly. "No. You claim that you have a conscience or at least something that keeps you from doing bad. What about dealing with the devil himself?"

Gina raised her eyebrows. "I should have known you would have found out about that. At the time, I was desperate. If I had it to do all over again, I would change things. It was stupid to be paid to traffic drugs."

"Drugs are only the half of it." Henry came closer to the door. He could hear quiet chatter coming from the vampires. "They are getting restless."

"What do you mean, drugs are only the half of it?" Gina ignored the restless comment. She knew that it was only a distraction, to keep her from continuing to ask questions. But she knew that asking questions and finding the answers was what had kept her alive this long.

Henry turned back to the vampire. "Do you really think I'd seriously tell you that?" Henry shook his head. "What information I do have Alicia will get if something should happen to me. And there is information about you that you wouldn't want that girl of yours finding out."

Gina shrugged. "I really don't think I can hide anything from her, not anymore. She already suspects most of what I was up to back then. It won't be long until she does figure things out. And that would be fine with me. After all these years, she deserves to know the truth."

"Including the truth about you?" Henry seemed genuinely surprised at the comment.

"By the time that this is all over, she'll know a lot of things she didn't know or want to know before." Gina eyed her enemy. "I'm guessing that would include things about you as well. And that damn organization of yours."

Henry simply nodded.

"Hello?" Ricky answered his vibrating cell phone.

"It's your boss. How go things?"

"Well, James, we are still waiting for any of them to show up." Ricky looked around at the antsy pack of vampires. "The fellas are getting kind of restless. We have orders that we can kill all of them, right?"

James sighed. "Yes, Ricky. But try and find out what those two know before you kill them. I want to know what information they have and how it could affect me and The Company."

"Sure thing." Ricky laughed nervously. "Am I going to be one of your key guys when all of this is said and done?"

"Just make sure not to screw this up." James' voice was filled with annoyance. "If anything should happen, you are the one that I am going to hold personally responsible. Do we truly understand one another?"

"Quite." The phone went dead. "Geez!" Ricky turned to the other vampires. "Listen. I want to be real clear on this. The boss wants us to first try and get as much information out of them as possible. After that, we can bleed them until they are dry. But if any of us screw this up, we'll be just memories."

"Are you sure this is the right way?" Alicia asked for the third time. "We've only got half an hour to get to Chez Pierre."

"We're almost out of this stinking place." Andrea pulled the strap of the duffle bag higher onto her shoulder. "We really need to get moving. I don't want them to discover that Adam is missing. Thank God Gina found him. I just wish I knew for sure if he were all right, It sounded real bad."

"Don't sweat it." Alicia put a hand on Andrea's back. "He's strong and young. He'll be able to pull through."

Andrea shrugged. "I'm sure you're right. I just wish I knew for sure." She flashed the flashlight around her. "Wait a minute." She walked over to a ladder. "This is the right place. I almost didn't recognize the exit. Someone's been playing with the bricks."

Alicia came over and looked at where Andrea was pointing the flashlight beam. "You're right. These four bricks look loose. Shall I?" Andrea nodded. Alicia took out all four stones. There were several plastic bags with a white substance inside. "I don't think that's powdered sugar inside."

"You can bet on that." Andrea flashed the light around some more. "There are more loose bricks. I'm wondering if this is like an underground trail for drug dealers." She watched Alicia put the bricks back in place. "I know these tunnels a little because of having to, on occasion, help out Gina. This is not her normal way of coming in and out. But there is a certain vampire I know that does use this tunnel."

"If not Gina, then who?"

Andrea smiled. "One of the smarmiest beings that ever graced the earth. He is a lackey of Gina's. That just may mean the two of them are in this together. Or maybe he's doing some things on his own."

"Or maybe he's working for somebody else." Alicia half smiled as Andrea turned to face her. "What if The Company is into drug dealing? I mean, it would explain why they would want us to quit asking so many questions. It would also explain why they were after

Gina so badly if she were trying to put an end to the drug trafficking. It makes you wonder what else they've been up to. What I was once a part of."

Andrea quickly moved within inches of her girlfriend. "You had no idea what they were up to. And you finally started to ask the right questions. That's why you are a good person. It finally clicked that things weren't as they seemed. Don't even put yourself in the same category as those creeps."

Alicia smiled. "Thanks. But I could have asked questions sooner. But we can't live in the past. We have to live in the present and hope for a bright tomorrow."

Andrea pulled her into a hug. "Let's go fight for our bright future together. I believe that together we can do anything."

Alicia smiled even brighter. "Now who's the optimist. Let's go kick some vampire ass and try and expose The Company for the creeps that they are."

"Somebody's coming." Gina and Henry quickly ducked into the linen closet across from the private dining room. Gina left the door open only a few inches. It was enough for her vampire eyes to see.

It was not long before she recognized the scent and the sight of Andrea. And there was that redhead that she had taken up with. She nodded toward the door. Henry peered out and nodded his recognition. Now all they had to do was wait until they had gone into the private dining room.

Andrea stopped in mid pace. Alicia looked at her questioningly. Andrea got a huge grin on her face. She pulled her in closer and whispered into the redhead's ear.

Alicia nodded and both continued to the private dining room. They had walked through the main restaurant. It surprised them both that it was open for business as usual. There were those there still enjoying a late breakfast or early lunch. In addition, there was the regular staff around.

"Ready?" Andrea whispered as she put her hand on the doorknobs of the double door. Alicia only nodded in response. Both entered without much fanfare. They looked around to see twenty vampires in a semicircle.

"You must be Miss Freemont and Miss Walker." A black with gold stripe haired vampire asked. He was on the short side.

"Hey, Ricky." Andrea smiled at the sudden look of fear on his face. "You don't remember me, but I remember you. You work for Gina. Or at least you used to."

"From time to time, yeah." Ricky straightened. The other vampires looked at him curiously as he readily admitted to working for the outlawed vampire. "We all got to do what we have to survive, now don't we."

"Some more than others." Andrea shook her head. "Give it up, Ricky. You can lie to your friends to make it sound better, but you are scared. So scared that you would do anything to come out on top. I've seen first hand what you are capable of. You know. You really should be more careful what you leave lying around in the sewers. Somebody less honest than me and my girl might think to profit from such things."

If it were possible, Ricky's face paled. He began squirming a little. "I haven't a clue as to what you're talking about."

Andrea shook her head. "Do you have any clue who you're talking to? I'm a detective. A damn good one at that. I've cracked some really tough cases. Ones that the expensive PIs are too scared to take on or not good enough. It didn't take much to realize you are probably screwing over whoever you're working with. I wonder what would happen if your partners ever found out. That'd be very interesting."

Nineteen sets of vampire eyes began staring at Ricky. He began squirming even more. "She's just trying to get you guys to not pay attention. Remember the orders. We're to do what we're told and not worry about anything else."

"When this is over," a small female vampire took two steps toward Ricky. "You may want to run for cover if you're not already out of the picture by then."

"That sounds like a good idea." All the vampires turned to look at the redhead, who had been quiet up until this point. "What? You think that she's the only one that speaks or knows anything. We're partners. In every sense of the word."

"Did you bring the paperwork like you were told?" Ricky still stood twitching considerably. "And where is Gina?"

"Not sure where the bitch is." Andrea took on the look of a betrayed friend. "Don't really care if she's blowing in the wind right now." She held out the little briefcase that she had been carrying. "This is all we know. I'm still not sure what everyone is getting so excited about. It makes me think that there is more to this than meets the eye."

"Perhaps if we survive this little fight, we will start doing a little digging." Ricky's eyes widened. "Whoops! Guess that wasn't the right thing to say." Alicia turned toward Andrea. "Looks like I really got us into a mess. I'm sorry, darling."

Andrea only smiled. "You only said what I was thinking. I've never been ale to let unanswered questions go on for too long. I'm the one that always has to solve the crossword puzzle. It always irritates me when I can't finish one. I think this puzzle is just about solved."

Ricky growled in his throat. His teeth elongated. "You two are really starting to irritate me." He walked over and grabbed the briefcase and then walked back to behind the semicircle of vampires. "I will be so glad when we can finish the job."

"If you're man enough to finish the job." Andrea smiled at his look of hatred. "But then, I've always found that a woman is much better at finishing some jobs."

"You are such a bitch." He opened the briefcase. He shook it upside down. A look of disgust came across his face as nothing fell out. "You two have really screwed each other over, do you know that? I can't believe how stupid the two of you really are."

"Or are we that smart?" Andrea took several steps toward the vampires. "You see, if something should happen to either of us, I've left instructions with a newspaper buddy of mine. He'll be more than happy to print the story that I've left for him. And what do you think would be bigger front cover news than The Company being sighted for illegal activities? After all, aren't they supposed to be a charitable organization?"

Ricky tore the briefcase to shreds. "You two." He sighed heavily. "I think the boss would agree that we have no choice in the matter. Kill the bitches." All nineteen vampires slowly moved in on Alicia and Andrea. Ricky stood back to watch.

Gina heard the entire conversation. She hoped that Andrea was just trying to bide time and make them think that they were not in league together. For their plan to work, it would have to appear that neither trusted the other.

Henry stood by her side. It was a strange feeling having to rely so heavily on her enemy for support. But these were the times that she lived in. Not a thrilling proposition putting the life of her charge in his hands, but his stepdaughter's life was also in the balance.

She eyed him carefully. They were waiting for the right moment to enter. She could feel the hatred almost burning off from him. If he were really on fire, she would be nothing but ashes by now. But she still could not blame him. Not being able to save his son was one of the things that still haunted her.

Not that he would believe that. Instead, he chose to think that she was evil. He probably only thought she was in this for whatever little bit she could gain, whether that gain was money, blood, or Andrea's friendship.

Finally, Henry noticed her staring. He rolled his eyes at her. She knew that he was irritated with her. But that would not stop him from doing what he had to. We all do what we have to, whether we like it or not.

A growl from inside caught both their attentions. As carefully as she could, she opened the doors a crack. Andrea was still laying it on thick and was really beginning to get to Ricky. And by the looks of the other vampires, they were not as trusting of their leader as they once were.

Gina smiled with pride watching her Andrea do her thing. She may now be able to take care of herself, but Gina would always be there watching out for her whether the woman wanted her to or not. The ripping of leather again brought her out of her thoughts. She watched as all the vampires except Ricky made their way toward Andrea and Alicia.

Henry was the first to enter. Gina stayed hidden behind the double doors. He walked up quickly to stand in front of the two women. "And what the hell is going on here?"

Ricky growled low in his throat. "What the hell are you doing here?" He took a couple steps toward the three humans. "You are no longer part of The Company. You are not supposed to be here. Although, it would be a bonus. You are on the list as well." The smile was almost pure evil.

"The hell I am." Henry stepped even closer to the vampires making their way toward him. "You kill me and there is going to be a lot of trouble. Kill these women and there'll be even more serious trouble. James will be none too trilled."

All the vampires froze in their tracks. "Don't be stupid!" Ricky took several more steps toward the humans. "He has been classified as a renegade longer than the two women have. James just kept him around so that he might be the fall guy should anything happen."

The vampires smiled at the thought. "You mean that it's time to start the dying?" A tall, muscular blonde male vampire practically growled.

"Do it!" Ricky said as he took several steps backwards.

All nineteen vampires launched themselves at the three humans. It was not long before the humans were all lying on their backs. Ricky smiled and leered. The thought of fresh human blood instead of those damn bags of blood that James always paid them in made his mouth water.

Before he could take two steps, one of the vampires trying to hold down Andrea turned to dust. "Well, at least I got rid of one of you soulless creatures." She struggled as four vampires pinned her shoulders to the ground. "What's the matter? It takes four of you to handle me? I wonder what would happen if it were one on one."

"Let's even the odds, shall we?" The strong female voice made all the vampires stop and stare. "What's the matter? You look like your worst nightmare has come true."

"Gina!" Ricky hissed her name. "You shouldn't have come here. You should just leave town while you can. The Company has assassins out looking for you now. If you were smart, you'd be on the run now."

"And if you were smart, you never would have crossed me." Gina launched herself in the air. She tackled the four vampires holding down Andrea.

Andrea quickly staked one of the vampires holding Alicia. The others backed off as Gina came toward them. The ones holding onto Henry also backed off. Now the four temporary allies stood watching the seventeen remaining vampires, not counting Ricky.

"We can do this the easy way or we can do this the hard way." Gina smiled at the looks she received. "Either way is fine by me. The results will be the same. All of you lackeys will be nonexistent before the next sunset."

"Attack them!" Ricky still stood back from the melee. He was slowly inching himself toward the back doorway.

"By all means, attack us." Andrea stood tall and proud between Alicia and Gina. Henry stood next to Alicia. All four waited still for the vampires to make the first move. "I think these guys don't really want to deal with us."

"I think you're right, sweetie." Alicia smiled. "We may just have to be the ones to make the first move."

"Anything is better then listening to this damn banter." Henry sighed heavily. "I know you're not an operative anymore, but couldn't you just for a little bit be professional about this? I mean our lives are at stake here. Would it kill you to be serious for two seconds?"

"Probably not." Andrea's eyes widened as the seventeen vampires finally started toward them. "But they might."

"Form a circle." Gina turned and now they all had their backs together. "Wait for them to make the first move."

As the vampires continued to slowly creep in, Andrea grabbed the duffle off her shoulder. "Shall we make this a little more interesting?" She pulled out four swords. Gina, Alicia, and Henry each took one from her. "I think that evens the odds just a little bit." The vampires froze. Gina shook her head. "This is ridiculous. I've never come across any vampires that are as afraid as you are. You have no conscience, and you have no heart. I have both. That's why I've survived as long as I have."

"Does that mean we take the fight to the scaredy cat vampires?" Alicia sounded a little scared.

"Let's just get this over with." Andrea went after the closest vampire, steadily swinging her sword. The vampire ducked and smiled. It did not realize that she had held a stake in her left hand and had made perfect use of it. "Bye, dust pile." She continued attacking and swinging her sword.

Alicia weakly swung her sword. One vampire ducked in time, but the one standing behind it was not so lucky. The sound of a head rolling on the ground gave her a sudden thrill. "Maybe this won't be so bad." That was when the vampire she missed punched her in the stomach, knocking out the wind from her lungs in the process. "Oh, crap!" she squeaked out.

Henry was standing beside her in two seconds. The offending vampire's dead heart met with a nice and sharp wooden stick. "Stay the hell away from my daughter."

Alicia smiled and mouthed thank you. "Look out!"

But it was too late. A vampire tackled Henry to the ground. Before Alicia could move to help, the sharp teeth were penetrating Henry's neck. Alicia moved to help, but there was suddenly only dust floating in the air. Gina smiled weakly before launching herself in the air.

Andrea had the sword knocked from her hand, and two vampires were about to take a little sample. All three were knocked to the ground. Gina staked one, and Andrea did the same to the other. She grabbed her sword as Gina helped her to her feet. "Thanks."

The odds were now four to eleven. Gina looked around the room. Ricky had done his usual thing and ran off to save his own skin. It was what he did. She knew it and still had tried trusting him.

Her mind was brought back into the present by a scream. Both Alicia and Andrea were pinned to the ground by seven vampires. Two were trying to get a hold of Henry. And two more stood in her path. She smiled at the thought.

The two in her way began shaking. She launched herself in the air, flipping over the two vampires. As she came down, she swiped her sword through the air and easily separating their heads from their bodies. She looked toward Henry. He had already dusted one of the two vampires. That still left Andrea and Alicia truly outnumbered.

Although, before she could move, that number dwindled by one. Still, she moved quickly. There were still six vampires. Alicia screamed again, but dust rained down on her face as she managed to get her arm free and stake the vampire.

Gina pulled two more stakes from the lining of her jacket. She somersaulted her way to where the remaining five vampires were terrorizing the two women were. Two more were easily taken out of the earthly realm. Andrea got to her feet, the sword in her hand. She swung with all of her might, making the three vampires headless.

Gina quickly turned to make sure that Henry was all right. Besides the blood dripping down his neck from where the one vampire she had dusted had gotten too close, he seemed fine. All nineteen vampires were toast.

"Was that all of them?" Andrea asked, her breathing was heavy still. Alicia came over and leaned her head on the sandy blonde's shoulder.

Gina shook her head. "I know that Ricky did his usual escape. But we took out these lackeys. I wonder how many more there are. And what about the human ones outside?"

Henry held up a hand. "I took care of them." Alicia raised her eyebrows. "I still had one of James' official looking documents and signed his name. They all think that the meeting was called off at the last moment. We've won. For now."

"You could have told us that." Gina smiled at the man. "So does this mean that we can possibly work together in the future?"

"Don't even go that far." Henry turned toward the door. When he got there, he turned back toward the three women. "Gina, I won't forget you saving my life. But I cannot and will not forgive the past. Don't ever ask me to and think I ever will." He turned and left.

"So what now?" Gina looked as the two lovers found a great deal of comfort from just the simple touch of the other. "What do we do now?"

Andrea smiled. "We have a little talk. But not now. Tomorrow. I want to check on Adam. But I do think the three of us need to talk."

The big battle had not taken as long as Andrea had thought it would. Not that she was complaining. She and Alicia were waiting for word on Adam in the busy emergency room. Now that she thought about it, the battle with the vampires was not what had her worried, it was the next move of The Company. What were they going to do now to keep them quiet?

"Miss Freemont?" A quiet female voice interrupted Andrea's thoughts. She and Alicia walked forward. "You're waiting on word about your employee, Adam Stevens?" Both women nodded. "Well, it's a good thing he got here when he did. Oh, I'm Doctor Rogers. I was wondering what happened to him."

Andrea shrugged. "I'm a private detective. I've been on a case for the last three days and haven't been in the office much. When I hadn't heard from him, I started checking the hospitals. Call it the pessimist in me. And in this business…"

"Do you have any enemies?" The doctor eyed the two women suspiciously. "This doesn't look like an accident."

"No actual enemy, but I haven't always gotten along with all the people I deal with." Andrea took Alicia's hand. She had been hurt a few times, battling vampires or other demons. It was always difficult explaining her injuries. But what Gina had described, it was like a torture thing. It would have to be the same explanation she hated using.

"Our last assignment was investigating the local gangs." Andrea did a half smile. "The ones that have been doing the rituals on all those victims. I had a couple clients that were worried about their teenagers. Perhaps I was getting a little too close and they wanted to send me a message. Is Adam awake?"

"He is still asleep. It will be a little bit before I believe he will wake up." Doctor Rogers did not look like she was buying her story. "Even though he's not awake, you can see him. Briefly. If he should wake up, call the nurse right away. I need to talk with him. This way."

Andrea and Alicia followed through the maze that was the ER. Adam still had not been taken to a room. He was behind one of the curtains in a filled to capacity ER. The bruises and cuts on his face were shocking.

"Again, don't take too long." Both women watched as the doctor made her way from the room.

"Damn!" Andrea came and sat by Adam's side. "This is all my fault. We were on the run, but I should have told Adam to do the same thing. Shit!"

Alicia came up and put a hand on her shoulder. "Things happened a little fast. I didn't think of warning him, either."

Andrea looked up at her girlfriend. "No offense, but I've worked with Adam for two years now. He's really a part of the team. I should have known."

A weak voice startled both women. "You couldn't have known." Adam's eyes fluttered open for a moment. But he quickly winced at the light and shut them again.

"You're just sucking up to the boss again." Andrea took Adam's hand in her own. "I'm sorry this happened. Do you know what happened?"

"Two men. Business suits. Blindfolded. Wanted you." Adam took a deep breath. It was clear that every word was causing him more and more pain.

"Don't talk." Andrea looked up at Alicia who nodded. "We think we know who did this. I'm so sorry. If I had warned you, you might not have gotten caught up in this. I'll understand if you quit. Don't worry about the hospital bills. They'll be taken care of." Andrea gently squeezed his hand.

Adam forced his eyes open for a moment. "Genuine affection. Concern." His words were still painful. "Red something else."

Alicia smiled. "Don't give me all the credit. She's an amazing woman in her own right. I just loosened her up a bit. I'll leave you two. I'll get a nurse or doctor."

Andrea watched her girlfriend walk toward the door. "When she gets here, you do know what to say about the attack, right?"

"Gang." Adam smiled. He winced at the pain it caused. He coughed several times. "Learned from the best."

"Wouldn't go that far." Andrea sighed. "I really am sorry about all this. And I'm going to warn you now, the danger's not over. It may never be over. Not as long as The Company is out there doing who knows what. Not until we can take them down. If you're still up for it."

"You're the boss." Adam sighed as well. "We will take them down. The three of us."

Gina paced back and forth under the sewer of the hospital. She wanted to know how Adam was doing. But she also wanted to give Andrea her space. It was a lot for anyone to take in. And now the woman's life would be in constant danger.

A deep male voice came from behind her. "I can't take it anymore." She turned to see Henry. He was armed with stakes, holy water, and a sword. "I can't believe you saved me. It has been tormenting me. But I believe you only did it for show. What is this sick twisted need you have for that woman, anyway?"

"I've been watching out for her ever since my mistake put her in danger." Gina took several steps toward the man. "It's what I do. I was even trying to look out for your son."

Henry cringed at her words. "You bitch! How dare you lie to me about Fredrick. There is no way in hell that you tried saving him. You are evil. All vampires and demons are evil."

Gina smiled. "That, dear Henry, is where you are terribly mistaken. The group of vampires I was working with back then were those that were left without consciences. You see, if you really want to know, when you become a vampire, you die. Your soul is released into the ether. Where it goes, depends on the life you have lived to that point. In its place, some receive a conscience which acts almost like a soul. Others, there is nothing but a void left. When your son died, his soul went where it went. But he was left without a conscience. He tried coming after me. I defended myself."

"You lying bitch!" Henry's face was growing red with anger. "My son would not choose to become a soulless creature as you. He was a good person. Unlike you."

Gina shrugged. She knew that any argument with him on this was useless. He believed what he believed to help him deal with his son's death. Even twenty years later, he would rather blame her than accept the truth. "I'm wondering how well you knew your son. Do you know what he was up to before he let himself be turned? Do you?"

"Shut up!" Henry took several dangerous steps toward the vampire. "I know all I need to know."

"If that were true, you wouldn't be here." Gina also took steps toward the man. "If you knew everything or believed some of the truth, you wouldn't be here. The death of your son was not my fault."

"Liar!" Henry began shaking with anger. "I can't listen to anymore of your lies." He suddenly raised a stake in his right hand and ran toward Gina. She easily dodged him and tripped him at the same time.

"You know that I can kill you in an instant." Gina looked down at the man, sadly. "Please don't make me."

"You kill because you want to." Henry quickly made it to his feet. He again charged her, this time his sword held tightly in his hands. Gina ducked his first swing, narrowly avoiding being decapitated. His second swing found her right arm with the follow through. She kicked the sword out of his hand. "Damn you!"

"Just walk away, Henry. Your stepdaughter still wants a relationship." Gina held her right arm with her left hand. The blood was flowing rapidly from the deep sword cut. "Be there for her now that you can't be for your son."

If it were possible, his face turned even redder. "I will have my revenge." He charged her again, managing to knock her to the ground. He was about to open the bottle of holy water and pour it on her when she bucked him off. He went flying. And landed on the sword that had landed upright.

"NO!" Gina rushed to his side. The sword had penetrated his heart. There was nothing that could be done. "I'm so sorry. I didn't want things to end like this. Damn!"

Henry coughed up blood. He stared into her dark eyes. "You finally got your wish. I'm dead, too. Tell Alicia I am proud of her. Not that it really matters to her." Gina watched in horror as his eyes rolled back in his head and his body went limp.

A growl echoed throughout the sewer. It echoed for several minutes. This was not what she had wanted. Death was never what she wanted. But it was a part of life, especially hers, the walking dead that she was. The next question, would Andrea believe this was all an accident, that she had tried to talk him out of this foolish duel? She turned quickly. She needed to find Andrea and tell her, tell her everything.

From the shadows of the sewers, a short figure emerged. The distinctive black hair with a gold striped man made his way toward the body. Smiling, he sunk his fangs into the body. If Gina were going to tell the woman that she had killed him, the best he could do was make it look like she had killed as a vampire would.

Wiping the blood from his face, he smiled. This could very well be the downfall of Gina. And then maybe this town would come under his control if he survived his meeting with James.

Andrea carefully opened the door to her office. Gina had called and sounded scared. That was something that she was not used to. Alicia followed her in. The place had been torn apart.

"I wonder if it's really safe to be here." Alicia picked up what was left of the computer from Adam's desk. "You do have insurance, don't you?"

Andrea half smiled. "Not exactly." Alicia raised her eyebrows. "They say I'm too high risk." The door to the office opened at that moment. "Gina!"

The female vampire was pale, even for her. There was blood on her hands. She looked down at the floor before looking back at Andrea and Alicia. "I have some terrible news." She turned toward Alicia. "I'm sorry, but Henry is dead. I-I tried to stop him, but he wouldn't not come after me. We struggled. He landed on a sword. There was nothing I could do to save him."

"Oh." Alicia tried to sound nonchalant. "His vendetta against you was going to be the end of him. I realized that."

"He…" Gina hesitated for a moment. "He did say he was proud of you. Those were his last words."

"Wow." Alicia made her way to behind Adam's desk and sat down. "I never thought he would say anything like that. I… " She looked at Andrea who quickly came over and gave her a kiss on the forehead. "I never thought he would ever say anything like that. It was always his son and not me."

"He was proud of you. Just like I am. You stood up for yourself. In the end, that's all we can do." Andrea could see the tears forming. "We still have each other. But The Company will probably be after us more than ever." She turned toward Gina. "Is that all you came to tell me?"

"No." Gina took two steps forward. "But now is not the time. You have much to deal with including the death of Henry and The Company."

Alicia looked up at the tall vampire. "The more we know, the safer we become. If we know their secrets, then someday we will be able to take them down."

"She's right." Andrea half smiled. "Adam almost lost his life because of whatever it is The Company thinks we know. And you were once a part of them, weren't you?" Her look had become almost fierce, she was so determined to learn the truth.

"I made some mistakes in the past." Gina sighed. "I was involved in their drug trade. I stole blood to pay vampires with fewer scruples. And I have taken human lives for them."

There was now shock on the face of Andrea. "You willingly took human lives? How could you? You always told me you were there to protect humans."

"I am, but these were people that were part of rival drug cartels." Gina began pacing. "Not that that makes any difference. Nor should it. They were still human. I went through a weak period before I saved your life. I did a lot of things I am not proud of. And your father was one of them."

Andrea raised her eyebrows. "I know he was part of the drug dealing or at least I think he was. What do you have to do with my father?"

"I'm the one that got him involved. He was the one that discovered my thefts of blood. It's what lead him to the other things I did." Gina stopped pacing and looked deep into her eyes. "If it weren't for me, he may not have gotten involved with James. But he did. He got greedy. That is why James sent those vampires after him. If I hadn't found out, you would be dead, too. I at least saved you."

Andrea stood taller. "This is a lot for me to take in. Are you sure that this is all that you want to tell me?"

Gina shrugged. "There is more to tell. There will probably always be more to tell. That's what happens when you've lived as long as I have. The past always comes back to haunt you." She looked at Andrea and Alicia. "No matter what you two decide to do, I will always be there looking out for you two. The Company is more dangerous now that they know you have even an inkling about what is going on. And of course, they know that I know many of their secrets. Hopefully, you'll be able to get past all of my past sins, and we can at least work together to expose them for who they are." She quickly turned and disappeared into the main office again.

Both Andrea and Alicia stared after the dark-haired vampire. She had pretty much confirmed all of their suspicions that they had. But the problem was, all the information that they had was all second hand. No eyewitnesses were available. None of what they had would hold up in court. And Andrea knew that none of her newspaper buddies would touch a story that could so easily be shot full of holes, especially about an organization that was so well respected. That threat had been useless.

Alicia stood and brought Andrea into a tight hug. She whispered in her ear. "We've uncovered a lot. About The Company, your father, Gina, and each other. But there is still so much to learn. We need to learn."

Andrea sighed. "And I'm still not sure if I can trust Gina. She says it was all in the past." She pulled back from the embrace. "We have a lot of work to do. We need to keep working for those that can't always afford the help. And those that are dealing with the supernatural. We need each other."

"That's what I was trying to say." Alicia smiled and kissed her girlfriend. She looked around the room. It was a total disaster area. "And don't worry about insurance or money. I want to invest in you, in us."

"What are you talking about?"

"Well, let's just say that I was really well paid by The Company." She shrugged. "I think it would only be fitting that I use that money to help take them down. We'll take money from those that can truly afford it, but we'll always be all right."

"As long as we stay together." Andrea leaned in for a long kiss. "I so want to take these guys out. They corrupt everything they touch. I don't want to see anymore people like you corrupted by these assholes. They prey on the young and the weak. The ones that haven't got hope. We will be there for those that need somebody to lean on. And cut off their supply of more operatives in the future."

James stared at the cowering vampire. Things had not gone well at all. Indeed. He had lost most of his vampire lackeys, which meant he would have to start from scratch. And good help was just so hard to find.

"But Henry is dead, and the vampire killed him." Ricky nodded in response to the question. "Well at least you didn't bungle that up."

James came quickly toward the vampire. "Tell me why I shouldn't replace you permanently? Is there any particular reason?"

"I did you a little favor." Ricky, still shaking, stepped a little toward the tall man.

"What kind of favor? Usually your favors are not of the good. I better be happy with this one." James' eyes did not leave the vampire.

"I-I made it so that when Henry's body is discovered, they might just think it was gang related." Ricky smiled at the amused look on James' face. "Andrea and Alicia may very well think that Gina killed Henry defending herself. But why would she then drain all of his blood?"

James smiled. "For once, you have indeed come through. Leave now. Start rounding up more of your kind. We will need to start after the two lesbians. They need to be silenced once and for all. Any way possible."

"I know of just the ones..." James held up a hand, cutting off Ricky's ranting. He nodded and turned and quickly left without another word.

James sighed heavily. He was startled by a male voice coming from behind him. "You really have botched this one, haven't you James?" Kirk stepped out of the shadows of the office.

"Kirk, you startled me." James took a step away from the senior man. The look on his face was pure evil.

Kirk smiled big. "As I should, James. You really are too stupid to get it. I run The Company the way I see fit. The others all fall in line. Unlike you, they don't want to admit to their wrong doings. You had fallen in line. And you are very creative in keeping the money coming in, any way possible. But now, you are getting careless. At one time, the two women would be nothing more than fertilizer in a cemetery. But now, they are still running around. And they have knowledge of some of your past discretions. And those discretions will only lead them to find out what The Company has been up to all these years." He shook his head in disappointment.

"I can and will fix things." James stood tall. "I know this town, and I know those two. And that vampire won't be a part of their team.

I have it all worked out. All you have to do is have a little faith. There is no stopping The Company. We will be grand again."

Kirk shook his head. "The only reason you are still in charge here is because you do know the people here. You seem to garner a nice respect from them. But you are weak. I hate to keep repeating myself, but it is the truth. You don't know when to put the final nail in the coffin. Someday that nail will be going in your coffin if you continue on this path. I may just personally see to that."

James sighed. He knew there was no arguing. He was lucky to still be in charge. After all, it was not that long ago that Henry had been his superior. And look how easy it had been to dethrone him. And Henry was now dead. If he was not careful, he would be the next victim on the long list of The Company. A list that he had help to add to over the many years of his long service to The Company.

"I will fix things. I guarantee you that." James took several steps toward Kirk. He pushed his fear aside and tried to show the confidence he once had. "I already have my connections rebuilding our network. It won't be long until everything returns to normal."

"Normal isn't what I was looking for." Kirk also stepped closer. The confidence he exuded was not forced. He knew he was in charge and to be feared. "I was looking for bigger and better things." He turned his back on James. "The Company wants to grow. Hopefully, you can learn to grow with them. If not, you can easily be replaced, just as Henry was."

James watched Kirk walk out the door. The writing on the wall was clear. He had to stop Andrea and Alicia, kill Gina, and take their operation to the next level. And as quickly as he could. Or he would be the one pushing up daisies in some cemetery.

Printed in the United Kingdom
by Lightning Source UK Ltd.
103665UKS00001B/71

9 781413 756029